Praise for Leonard Sanders's *The Hamlet Warning*

"EXCITING, SUSPENSEFUL, AND HAS A MAN'S MAN OF A HERO. . . . LOOMIS IS AS TOUGH A KILLING MACHINE AS INTERNATIONAL SKULDUGGERY HAS TO OFFER."

—*The New York Times Book Review*

"HIGH ADVENTURE, MARVELOUSLY TOLD . . . IT HAS THE RING OF COMPLETE AUTHENTICITY."

—Robert Ludlum

"ONE OF THE BEST . . . A TRULY HAIR-RAISING DENOUEMENT."

—*Boston Globe*

"A PLOT FULL OF CAPTIVATING TWISTS."

—*Time*

"A GENUINE THRILLER, GROWING IN THE INTENSITY OF ITS EXCITEMENT TO THE VERY LAST PAGE."

—Irving Stone

"THE FINAL 30 PAGES ARE ABOUT AS SWEATY AS ANY THRILLER EVER WRITTEN."

—*San Diego Union*

"THE KIND OF ADVENTURE THE OTHER GUYS WERE ONLY TRYING TO WRITE."

—*Seattle Post-Intelligencer*

Books by Leonard Sanders

The Emperor's Shield
The Eternal Enemies
The Hamlet Ultimatum
The Hamlet Warning

Published by POCKET BOOKS

The Eternal Enemies

LEONARD SANDERS

POCKET BOOKS
New York London Toronto Sydney Tokyo Singapore

This book is a work of fiction. Names, characters, places and incidents are either products of the author's imagination or are used fictitiously. Any resemblance to actual events or locales or persons, living or dead, is entirely coincidental.

An *Original* Publication of POCKET BOOKS

POCKET BOOKS, a division of Simon & Schuster Inc.
1230 Avenue of the Americas, New York, NY 10020

ISBN: 0-671-67273-8

First Pocket Books printing October 1991

10 9 8 7 6 5 4 3 2 1

POCKET and colophon are registered trademarks of Simon & Schuster Inc.

Printed in the U.S.A.

The individual soul is unbreakable and insoluble, and can be neither burned nor dried. It is everlasting, all pervading, unchangeable, immovable, and eternally the same.

—*Bhagavad-Gita*

The Eternal Enemies

1

Twice Loomis heard the snick of a rifle bolt. The sound was unmistakable despite being muffled by heavy snow swirling down through the Himalayan pass. He put out a hand, seized Owenby by the shoulder, and pushed him into the protection of an overhang. Winded from the altitude and the last long, steep climb, he spoke low in Owenby's ear.

"Someone's up there. In the pass. Waiting for us. They're armed."

Owenby gave him a calm, appraising stare. His slate-blue eyes were half hidden behind the slit in his protective face mask. But he did not complicate matters by asking stupid questions, and Loomis liked that. Instead, Owenby put up a heavily gloved hand. The line of yaks and Gurkha porters behind them stopped. A few of the drivers immediately sought shelter from the wind amidst the twists in the narrow trail.

Owenby's eyes remained serene, but he spoke with all of his upper-crust British disdain. "Someone in the pass, you say? Is there now? That's interesting. Who are the buggers do you suppose?"

"I have no idea," Loomis said. He described the sounds of the rifle bolts.

Owenby peered ahead through the snow. "Bugger all! We can't go forward. We can't stay here. Night's coming on. Temperatures here will drop sixty degrees. So there you are. We'll bloody well have to go back, old sod. Not much choice, that. We'll be damned lucky if we make it. You do follow me, don't you?"

Loomis did. They were on the longest and most dangerous stretch of this route over the Himalayas. In early afternoon an unseasonable, early fall storm had swept down on them. The last shelter was now ten hours behind them—an impossible distance in darkness at sixty below zero, especially after a grueling day and with exhausted animals. The only safety lay three hours ahead, through the pass and to the next shelter. They had to reach it before night fell.

It was a tight situation, and Loomis found no comfort in the fact that Owenby was an unknown quality, hired by a person even more obscure to smuggle Loomis through Nepal, over the roof of the world, and into western Tibet.

In the three weeks they had been together, Loomis had been unable to learn much about Owenby. The man was talkative, and full of information on every subject except himself. Loomis had assembled only a few tidbits: Owenby once had lived in Hong Kong. He had taken a degree at Trinity College at Oxford and was English to the core. Now Loomis wished he had made an effort to learn more. The only source at his disposal in Kathmandu had dismissed Owenby out of hand as a minor rogue trader and sometime gunrunner. Loomis suspected he was much more.

Loomis had not bothered to investigate the goods Owenby was bringing into Tibet with his caravan of fourteen yaks, but he assumed guns were a part of the manifest. He could not condemn Owenby for that. Utilizing his old CIA skills, Loomis himself had smuggled a .380 Smith & Wesson automatic through customs at Kathmandu. It now resided in a special holster under his heavy coat.

Thinking back to the sounds in the pass, he had no doubt of what he had heard. Years of experience had taught him to trust his first impression. He was certain the snicks had come from a bolt-operated rifle, possibly an old Springfield or Krag, but probably some type of Mauser. The sound had been faint and far away. But the scrape of a rifle bolt ramming home a cartridge was like no other.

And he had no doubts about the situation. The people waiting in ambush had heard the approach of Owenby's caravan and worked their bolt actions on their rifles to confirm that they were not frozen.

"You have any thoughts on who it could be?" he asked Owenby.

"Oh, bandits, I'd suppose. Quite a few of them operating in this part of the world."

Owenby's eyes tended to protrude, showing a lot of white. Loomis estimated he was in his late thirties or early forties. He was tall and lanky, yet graceful in movement, and he had lengthy, prominent dark eyelashes that fanned out, giving him an expression of constant surprise. But Loomis had found that nothing much surprised Owenby, who now gazed with an almost disinterested casualness toward the pass.

"It could be that the buggers want my cargo. Or you. I don't know." He spat on the rocks, testing the temperature by watching his saliva freeze. "Jesus! Look at that! We can't stay here. We best start back. Even if we hurry, we bloody well might not make it."

"Can you unpack one of whatever it is you're carrying?" Loomis asked. "And a few rounds of ammunition?"

Owenby turned to look at him. "Bugger you, old sod. You've been into my packs."

"No. But I did take the trouble to check out your

reputation back in Kathmandu. They said you run guns. Right now, the only chance I see for us is to break out some guns and clear that pass."

"Hadn't you noticed? I'm not one of your cinema cowboys. Don't expect me to charge the buggers."

"I didn't ask you to. All I want is a weapon."

Owenby hesitated only briefly. He turned and went back down the trail a dozen steps to where one of the Gurkha tribesmen waited. While they conversed in a hill-country dialect, Loomis studied the terrain ahead.

The narrow trail clung to the side of a mountain, high over a gorge that stretched away to unseen depths below. Across the way, the other side of the gorge could be seen faintly through swirling snow. The pass was not high for this part of the world—hardly more than nineteen thousand feet—but the climb for the next several hundred yards was steep through scattered boulders.

Owenby had said this route had been used for centuries by smugglers and salt traders operating between Nepal and Tibet. He had said it was now safer for clandestine operations because it was well removed from the principal trade centers and rarely used. Earlier in the day they had seen some of the highest peaks of the Himalayas. But with the arrival of the snowstorm more than two hours ago the sky had lowered. Now even the pass ahead was obscured.

Loomis pulled down the ear flaps of his cap, shivered, and thought back to the mystery of the letter that had enticed him into this part of the world. He wondered who was in the pass and what adventures lay ahead for him in Tibet—assuming he could get there.

The letter had come to him at his home in Beverly Hills. It was written on ancient parchment in an elaborate script.

My Dear Mr. Loomis,

Long search has brought me to you. Your talents could prove of lasting benefit to myself, to many oppressed people, and perhaps to all mankind.

Since the task I am asking you to perform will be difficult and dangerous in the extreme, we are prepared to pay twice your usual fee. I implore that you contact Mr. Bertrand Owenby in Kathmandu, discreetly and in person. He will escort you to me. Please be prepared for a lengthy journey. If after our talk you are not inclined to accept the task, we will of course recompense you well for your trouble.

Sincerely,
Lhalde Phakpa

That had been all. In many ways the letter contained nothing to distinguish it from an abundance of crackpot lures that frequently came to Loomis, as they did to most everyone who hired himself out as a mercenary. Usually such requests led to someone who wanted to do away with someone else in an elaborate plot for a profit. Sometimes they led to someone convinced that Adolf Hitler's stolen gold lay buried in a Brazilian tin mine or that a gold horde buried by President Ferdinand Marcos still reposed somewhere in the Philippines, lying there for the taking.

Through the years Loomis had received dozens of similar mysterious requests for his talents. He had investigated some, even been tempted by a few.

But this one carried a subtle ring of authenticity.

Plainly the sender had done his research. "Of lasting benefit . . . to many oppressed people" was a phrase well chosen to snare Loomis's interest.

And how could he possibly be of benefit "to all mankind"? That line also was right on target.

But it was the phrase "difficult and dangerous in the extreme" that had convinced Loomis that the sender had done his homework.

The challenge might have raised the flag of caution among most of the men in Loomis's profession. But the sender apparently had known that Loomis would be drawn irresistibly by the promise of danger.

The letter could not have come at a better time.

Loomis's Maria Elena had just left for location shooting in Spain for the first film role she had accepted since the facial injuries she had received in terrorist bombings almost a year ago. Understandably, she was nervous about returning to the cameras, and she had never liked distractions such as a husband while she was working.

Moreover, Loomis was tired of the complexities and double-dealings common in working with governments and political groups. This assignment sounded like a welcome diversion.

Following the instructions in the letter, he had gone to Kathmandu. There he had checked into the Yak and Yeti on Durbar Marg, the main thoroughfare. As a precaution, he had spent several days blending with the tourists on excursions to Bhaktapur and Patan. But quietly he made discrete inquiries of Bertrand Owenby, describing him as "a friend of a friend."

At last word had reached Owenby, who had left a note at the Yak and Yeti inviting Loomis to dinner at Sherpaland, a restaurant on the seventh floor of the Everest Sheraton. There, at the highest point in the valley, with a sweeping view of the Himalayas, they had met over superb Tibetan-Mongolian dishes. In subsequent meetings over the next two days, they made plans for surreptitious entry into Tibet.

The meeting with Owenby had been a strange experience. Owenby stoutly claimed that he had been hired only to escort Loomis into Tibet and that he was unaware of any "task." He said he was not yet authorized to discuss his relationship with his client, but that Loomis would know all in good time. He said their journey to the rendezvous with Lhalde Phakpa would require from a month to six weeks of hard travel.

Reluctant, yet hopelessly intrigued, Loomis at last agreed to go.

After outfitting in Kathmandu they had set out. On the edge of the Himalayas Owenby had paused for two weeks while he put Loomis through a rigorous physical course to get him acclimated to the altitude.

For a simple smuggler, Owenby seemed to possess a vast store of medical knowledge.

"Mind you, even at seventeen thousand feet each lungful of this bloody air has only half as many molecules of oxygen as what you'll find in your peaceful bed back in Beverly Hills. Half! You'll learn you've been drowning in oxygen all your life and didn't know it. For a while up there you'll be as sick as a Piccadilly whore. Your body simply can't pump enough oxygen into your lungs, or process it. The rotting buggers who live at this altitude have almost twenty-five percent more oxygen-carrying hemoglobin in their blood than you or I. They're born with it. And there you are. We'll never match them. But by training our bodies we can build a little more hemoglobin. Not much, but a little."

After the two-week delay they had traveled into a remote region of the Himalayas and from there turned northward, climbing through the mountains toward Tibet.

As yet, Owenby would not reveal exactly where they were going.

Now, apparently, some of the "danger in the extreme" mentioned in the letter had made its appearance.

Loomis did not know its nature, and Owenby clearly was being less than candid.

Loomis was not at all happy with the situation.

Owenby returned with a rifle and an ammunition box. "This is the best of the lot, old sod. I'm assuming you know how to use it."

Loomis gave the weapon a quick examination. It was a Romanian copy of the Kalashnikov AKM. He checked the action, the bore. It was chambered for the 7.62 M43 cartridge. The rifle had been used. But it had received good care.

Loomis removed a glove, knelt in the snow, and inserted ammunition into three banana clips.

"Anything I could be doing while you're having your jollies up there?" Owenby asked.

"Just stay here and make a little noise from time to time."

Owenby again glanced toward the head of the pass. "Remember, old sod, I'm not lingering here long. Even the bloody yaks will freeze. I won't wait for you."

"Give me an hour," Loomis said.

"Dear boy, I don't have an hour to give. Unless we find shelter soon, we're all dead."

Loomis lost patience.

"You should have thought of that before you came up here without the proper equipment. We can't possibly make it back and you know it. The only way out is ahead, through that pass. Wait twenty or thirty minutes, then start making a little noise, like you're having trouble adjusting the loads. Not too much. Just enough to let them know you're still here."

Not waiting for a reply, Loomis turned and walked back down the trail, past the yaks and the Gurkha handlers.

The yaks were standing quietly, with heads lowered against the snow. They were ungainly beasts, resembling a cross between shaggy goats and American buffalo. But they could carry up to two hundred pounds all day without tiring, and they thrived on altitude. Owenby claimed that if a yak was taken below thirteen thousand feet it became sickly, went into a rapid decline, and would die unless given special attention.

Choosing his place, Loomis slung the Kalashnikov on his right shoulder and started climbing the sheer wall of the mountain. Handholds were few, and snow was caked into every crevice. Slowly Loomis labored upward, taking his time, aware that a single slip would be his last.

Every yard gained seemed to take all of his strength. Nausea swept through him in waves. Every few yards he stopped and gasped for air.

Soon the trail, the gorge, the pass were lost in the swirling snow. He could see only the rocks and boulders within reach.

Owenby had been right about the temperatures; already the wind was growing colder. At every opportunity, Loomis worked his feet inside his heavy boots to preserve circulation. Every time he stopped for breath he put his heavily gloved hands beneath his coat, under his armpits, in an effort to keep his fingers from freezing.

Gradually he edged to the right, trying to estimate distances. Several times he was forced to climb higher, or to drop lower, to skirt outcroppings of rock. His lungs felt as if they were about to burst from the exertion.

At last, after a half hour of maneuvering, he judged that he was over the pass. Slowly, taking great care not to make a sound, he began his descent.

He was hoping the ambushers would be watching the trail below, not expecting anyone to drop down on them from out of the clouds.

As he eased lower, the pass, the other side of the gorge gradually took vague shape. He halted, braced against the wind, and listened.

He heard no sound and saw no movement.

He moved lower. Again he stopped.

In the midst of the swirling snow a man assumed shape about thirty yards away. He was in a prone position, his rifle aimed down the trail.

Cautiously, Loomis edged closer. From down the trail came the creak of a saddle girth, the scrape of a hoof on rock.

Abruptly the man rolled onto his right side and raised his left arm three times in a signal. On the opposite side of the gorge, barely visible, three forms moved to a lower elevation. There they took up new positions.

Loomis estimated the range to the farthest man at just under two hundred yards. He pushed the selection lever of the Kalashnikov to full automatic. Using a small boulder as a rest, he brought the sights to bear on the distant form, almost obscured from time to time by the wind-driven snow.

Slowly Loomis squeezed the trigger.

The roar of the explosion filled the pass, echoing from one side to the other.

Firing short bursts, shifting targets, Loomis shot the three men on the other side of the pass.

The man below, the one who had done the signaling, reacted with surprising speed. He turned and got off a shot before Loomis rolled to one side and fired a burst into him.

A barrage of bullets came from across the gorge and struck close about Loomis. Still rolling, half falling, Loomis moved twenty yards down the slope and to the right. The firing continued, the bullets thudding into his previous location.

Loomis lay quiet. In the falling snow he barely could make out the faint red winks of two muzzles. Still he waited. The two red winks were repeated. There were no others.

Loomis took careful aim and returned fire. The guns fell silent.

He lay motionless for several minutes. Nothing stirred except wind and snow.

He would have preferred further caution, but the choice was between risking a bullet and freezing. Rising from cover, he walked down the slope to where the trail went through the pass.

No more shots were fired.

He put a boot under the corpse beside the trail and rolled it over. Already it was growing stiff, an arm upraised, frozen into one last signal. The face was Oriental, perhaps Mongolian. Yet there was something different about his features.

Loomis did not bother to cross the gorge to see about the others. He put down his rifle, cupped his gloved hands to his mouth, and shouted down the trail.

"Owenby! Come on up! All clear!"

While waiting for Owenby, Loomis searched through the man's pockets. Except for forty rounds of 7mm ammunition, they were empty.

He picked up the man's rifle. It was an ancient Spanish 1892 7mm Mauser.

Owenby and his caravan came on up the trail. When Owenby reached him, Loomis pointed to the body.

"Know this fellow? He seemed to be the leader."

Owenby gave the body only a glance and shook his head. "No. Can't say I do."

Loomis was certain Owenby was lying.

He persisted. "What is he? Tibetan? Nepalese?"

Owenby did not appear remotely interested, a stance Loomis found odd under the circumstances.

"Can't really say. He could be Chinese. Maybe Tibetan. Odd-looking sod. Hard to tell. But we'd best be off, old chum, if we're to make that shelter before dark."

Loomis pointed across the gorge. "There are five others over there. No easy way to bury them up here. But maybe they should be tumbled off into the gorge. The Nepalese army might get curious over who's been littering up their pass."

Owenby shouted orders. Two of his yak handlers began the descent to the frozen stream below. In a surprisingly short time they were climbing the opposite slope. Then the bodies came tumbling down, one by one, and dropped into the gorge.

With the temperatures at this altitude well below freezing even through the summers, the bodies might be preserved indefinitely.

Only now did Loomis have time to reflect on his altered situation. He had come this far uncommitted, fully prepared to refuse if the "task" he was asked to perform was not to his liking. But now, with the shootout and six men dead, he was on dangerous ground. He was traveling without papers, accompanied by an arms smuggler, and he had just killed six citizens of some country or other.

He still had no inkling of exactly who had requested his services or for what. Was the ambush part of the "extreme" danger his prospective client had promised? Or were the six men simple bandits, as Owenby had suggested?

Loomis felt he deserved answers. He took Owenby to one side.

"Look, I've just killed six men and I don't even know who the hell they were. I think it's high time you leveled with me."

Owenby watched the last corpse tumble into the ravine. He glanced up at the sky, as though trying to estimate through the snow how much daylight remained.

"Right you are, old sod. But I was told to bring you over the Himalayas before I filled you in. We simply must get moving. Tonight, when we reach the shelter, I'll tell you all I know. And that's a bloody promise."

2

"Are you familiar with the Chang Tang?" Owenby asked.

Loomis considered the question. He knew that was the common label for the Tibetan high plateau.

"Only in a general way," he said.

Loomis and Owenby were seated in the corner of a one-room stone and mud hut. Outside, the wind still howled. Inside, warmth was beginning to build. Heavy smoke drifted upward from the yak-manure fire and disappeared through a vent in the roof. Pushing the animals, they had descended from the pass and reached the hut an hour after darkness. They had eaten—yogurt, a strange salted, buttered tea, and a roasted barley flour cake called *tsamba.*

Already Owenby's six Gurkhas were bedding down for the night. But Owenby had broken out a bottle of Boodles gin and made himself comfortable on his bedroll by the fire.

Loomis wondered if Owenby was even younger than he appeared. He showed no signs of fatigue after the long, difficult day.

"Mind you, the Chang Tang—the Tibetan high plateau—is probably the most remote region left on the face of the earth," Owenby said conversationally. "And that's where we're headed. Way to the hell and gone onto the high Tibetan plateau."

Loomis sipped his gin and grimaced. It was not a good chaser for yogurt. "*How* far, exactly?" he asked.

Owenby reached into a pocket of his quilted coat and unfolded a map. He spread it across his knee and pointed. "About six hundred miles from where we sit, old chum. Deep into the far western portion of the plateau. I'm sorry if I trucked you about a bit over our destination. But the truth is that my instructions were to bring you to this hut before telling you a bloody thing. Now I can tell you as much as I know. Then, if you decide this isn't your lot, I'm to arrange safe transportation for you back to Kathmandu. And here it gets tricky. I must have your decision by morning in order to make the arrangements."

Loomis thought of the six dead men in the pass. If the bodies happened to be discovered, the authorities in Nepal would have little difficulty in putting it all together. Every trader in Kathmandu would know that Owenby had gone into the Himalayas escorting an American. Loomis had no doubt but that he would soon be identified. An unsavory situation might be awaiting him back in Kathmandu.

"I need a hell of a lot more information before I can make a decision," Loomis said. "All I know thus far is that I received a letter signed Lhalde Phakpa, with no return address, asking that I contact you. Just for starters, who's Lhalde Phakpa?"

Owenby placed his glass of gin on the fireplace stones and warmed his hands over the dung fire. "I'll tell you in a moment. But first, so you'll really understand, you've got to know about the general situation in Tibet. Are you aware of what's been happening to that poor bloody country during the last few years?"

Irritated by the continuing quiz, Loomis did not answer.

"It's interesting, and at the same time a damned tragedy," Owenby said. "And it's all but unknown to the outside world. Not like your Tiananmen Square, where that young sod stood up to the Red tank and had his picture played on everybody's telly all over the globe. People wept buckets. Widespread indignation, condemnation. But here in Tibet the same bloody Red Chinese have destroyed an innocent country, murdered thousands, and the world has looked the other way. Thank you bloody much and there you are."

Owenby was growing drunk and even more loquacious. Loomis was vaguely familiar with the course of events in Tibet, but he did not remember the details. He listened quietly as Owenby continued.

"Until it was invaded by Red China in 1950, Tibet was the last true theocracy on this planet and probably the most religious-minded country in the world. First rattle out of the box, the Chinese closed the monasteries. They outlawed religion, all religious ceremonies. Funerals even!"

Again Owenby spread his map and pointed. "The high plateau—where we're going—is roughly a thousand miles long, six hundred miles wide. When the Red buggers took over the country, there wasn't a single road or railroad from Lhasa on westward. Not in this whole region. It's boxed in by the Himalayas on the south and west, by China on the north and east, and cut off from the bloody world. Not a tree, not even what you could call a bush grows there. Nothing on the whole plateau but grass, lakes, rocks, sand, and mountains you bloody well have to see to believe. It's forbidding country. But oddly beautiful, for all that."

Loomis found himself making a new appraisal of Owenby. Under the influence of the gin and the growing warmth of the hut, Owenby at last was going beyond his subject to reveal something of himself.

"Out on that plateau, when the Chinese came, there were maybe two hundred thousand *drokba*—nomads—living in that great vastness the same way they've been living since Christ was a tadpole. I say two hundred thousand. But really, nobody knows how many. So how in bloody hell were the Red buggers to subdue them? Why, they had to build roads to them. So they put the Tibetans to work. Understand, one-fifth of all the males in Tibet were Buddhist monks, and they'd always been exempt from conscription. But no longer. The Red buggers put them to work, building bridges over the chasms, digging tunnels, what have you. Worked the poor blokes to death. Thousands died. In 1959, here in the most peaceful country in the world, there was a revolt. It failed. The Dalai Lama was at that time more or less the head of the country. He fled into exile in India. Thousands upon thousands were killed. No one knows how many."

Loomis remained silent. He was vaguely familiar with the series of events Owenby described.

"But the Red buggers got their roads built. A highway along the southern edge of the plateau, then back through the middle, completed just in time for the big Chinese Cultural Revolution of 1969. The Red army came, riding in their bloody lorries. The *drokba* were rounded up and put into communes. Their herds were taken from them. For ten years they damned near starved. Then in 1980 the Chinese finally admitted that the communes weren't working worth a damn. The *drokba* were restored to family groups. Now they've returned to their old ways. I tell you this because that's where we're going. Among the *drokba.*" He pointed to the map. "They live in this region throughout the year at elevations from sixteen to eighteen thousand feet. They're the highest resident population in the world."

Loomis was still wondering what the hell all this had to do with the "task" he had been invited here to perform. Owenby leaned forward over the dung fire and lit a cigarette.

"How much do you know about Buddhism?" he asked.

"Not nearly as much as you're dying to tell me," Loomis said.

Owenby laughed. "Well, there isn't much more, old sod. But you bloody well need to know the context to make your decision. Don't you see, Tibet has been devoutly Buddhist since the thirteenth century. For eight centuries! The Dalai Lama is the fourteenth reincarnation of the Bodhisattva Avalokitesvara. Some people also know that there is—or was—a Panchen Lama, more or less the number two Tibetan ruler. He died a couple of years ago. I haven't heard if he's popped back into the world of the living again. What most of the world *doesn't* know is that there are hundreds of lamas. Reincarnations. Before the Chinese came, most had their own monasteries—or lamaseries, if you prefer—each with a devout following among the *drokba.* But the Communists bombed and destroyed the lamaseries, knocked down the prayer walls, outlawed Buddhism."

Owenby finished his cigarette in silence, then tossed it into the fire. He looked at Loomis and gave each word dramatic emphasis.

"Lhalde Phakpa, the man who wrote you that letter and who hired me, is abbot of the monastery of the Kamala Lama. Lhalde's a remarkable sod. As a young man he left Tibet, studied in Shanghai and at the University of Beijing. He was a Rhodes Scholar to Oxford. He took degrees up the ass. But after all of his studies, he returned to Tibet and the lamasery. When the Chinese destroyed their lamasery, Lhalde, his Kamala Lama, and his monks fled far into the western plateau. I don't know where." Again Owenby pointed to the map. "We're to meet Lhalde here, two hundred miles north and west of Lake Drabye. We're running a bit behind schedule. We'll have to travel hard to keep the rendezvous."

Loomis waited. But Owenby seemed to have run out of words.

"Exactly what are your connections with him?"

For a moment Loomis thought Owenby might refuse to answer. But after a brief hesitation, he seemed to reconsider.

"Well, for many years, I was banker and financial adviser for Lhalde and his monastery."

Loomis must have allowed his skepticism to show. Owenby took immediate offense. The gin not only had loosened his tongue, but was now slurring his speech.

"I wasn't always a gunrunner, old sod. Once I was president and chief executive officer of one of your larger banks in Hong Kong. Believe it or not, I had chauffeured limousines, and women, at my beck and call twenty-four hours a day. And you should have seen some of those women!" He shook his head sadly.

"What happened?" Loomis asked.

Owenby looked at him a long moment before answering. "I was too ambitious by half. London School of Finance, University of Basel doctorate. I was young and I knew it all. I tried to corner the market in cocoa bean futures. But something happened to the goddamned beans that year. I still don't know exactly what. Unfortunately, I had used bank money to bolster my position."

Loomis shook his head in commiseration. Owenby gave him a rueful shrug.

"I found it necessary for a change of residence, preferably to a country rather lax on the subject of extradition. I chose Nepal. I'm a businessman, so I became a trader. I kept in touch with a few clients, Lhalde among them. We understand each other. Old school ties, I guess. We're both Trinity, or did I tell you? He's aware that I'm basically an honest man, so he continues to employ me from time to time. There you have it, my entire story. It wasn't part of the deal. I throw it in free."

"What does he want with me?" Loomis asked.

Again Owenby shrugged. "I haven't the foggiest, old sod. My instructions were to bring you to this hut and to tell you all I know. I have done so. I suppose he'll tell you what it's all about when and if we get there. Assuming you wish to continue."

Loomis looked at the map. The roads built by the Chinese with forced Tibetan labor ran east and west. One lay along the southern edge of the region, the other through the central portion.

"What if the Chinese should happen to find us in Tibet?"

Owenby drew a forefinger across his throat. "The outside world would never know what happened to you."

Loomis frowned, studying the map. Why would a monastery need his services?

Surely a handful of monks did not intend to take on the whole Red Chinese army.

"One more question," he said. "Who was the corpse in the pass?"

Again Owenby hesitated. "That sod had nothing to do with this. I'm sure of it. He was after the rifles I'm transporting. Your being there was merely a coincidence."

"Then why can't I have his name?"

Owenby did not answer for a time. But at last he spoke reluctantly. "He was Takla Pishan, a man from the Xinjiang Province, just to the north of Tibet. I met him once in Kashi. I have no idea what the bugger was doing in Nepal. And that's the honest truth."

"What was his trade?"

"Guns. He sold mostly to the Uighur Muslims in Xinjiang Province. From time to time he bought a few old Mausers and Enfields from me, for the fighting in Pakistan and Afghanistan. That was three and four years ago. I hadn't seen him since."

Loomis examined the map. The Xinjiang Province lay only two hundred miles beyond where he was to meet Lhalde.

Maybe the ambush in the pass was not as much a coincidence as Owenby believed.

Owenby passed the gin bottle. Loomis declined. Owenby capped it and returned it to his luggage.

"We'd best be to bed. Long day and all that. But I'll need your decision first off in the morning, if not sooner.

We're to meet a caravan headed south. If you want to go with them, you must speak up."

"I take it you're bound for the rendezvous with Lhalde, with or without me."

"You might say that," Owenby agreed.

Loomis took one last look at the map. Contour lines throughout the high plateau showed areas of desertlike flatness interspersed among lakes and rugged mountains. He handed the map back to Owenby.

"I'll go on," he said. "At least the scenery looks interesting."

3

Gradually they came down off the Himalayan cordillera into stretches of vast, dry plain surrounded by snowcapped peaks. On the mountainsides, blue-tinged glaciers glittered in the sun. Occasionally they passed stupas—towerlike Buddhist shrines—beside the trail, but seldom did they see any sign of humans. If anything, Owenby had understated the remoteness of the region.

They passed well to the west of the town of Shigatse into a land where Loomis could discern no trail. But Owenby seemed to know where they were going.

The ground was covered with fist-sized rocks that made footing difficult. The yaks did not seem to mind but plodded along, looking first one way, then the other, in their peculiar manner. Most of the time Loomis and Owenby rode yaks, in deference to the altitude. Loomis felt foolish aboard the animals, for his stirrups had to be shortened drastically to prevent his feet from dragging the ground. As a consequence, he rode in a sort of squat, with his knees tucked up under his chin. But only twenty minutes of travel on foot was enough to leave him nauseated and panting, for they were still well above sixteen thousand feet. After several attempts, he surrendered to the inevitable, and remained in the saddle.

Owenby seemed to fare better with the altitude, but apparently saved his breath for talking. He usually rode beside Loomis, and obviously considered himself a self-appointed tour guide. He pointed to the surrounding mountains.

"Interesting geology here. India used to be a separate continent, don't you know, like Australia. Drifted north fast and slammed into Asia only yesterday, geologically speaking. That's what caused all this. Buckled the landforms like old cardboard. And there you are. The Himalayas, these mountains, the whole bloody plateau, created by the pressures of continents colliding. Still going on. The region drives seismographs crazy. Thousands of shocks a day. Geology turned upside down. Some of the prettiest conch shells you'll ever see can be found in shops in Kathmandu. Know where they find them?" Again Owenby pointed. "Top of the Himalayas. Parts of those mountaintops were below the ocean not long ago. Can you imagine?"

Owenby seemed to consider himself an authority on most every subject and was more than willing to share his expertise. Loomis often welcomed darkness and bed with the hope of giving his ears a rest.

They set a fast pace. Occasionally the Gurkhas complained. Loomis inferred from their gestures and expressions that they were protesting to Owenby that he was driving both them and the animals too hard. Owenby did not relent.

That afternoon they came to the first sign of civilization since Kathmandu: the narrow road the Red Chinese had built across the high plateau. Of dirt and gravel, it was not impressive. Loomis reflected that back in his home state of Texas it would not even qualify as a good county-line road.

Owenby halted the caravan and watched for a time.

Nothing moved along the road, but Loomis could see that Owenby was worried.

"Not a bloody cloud in the sky, and a full moon rising before sunset," he said. "And we can't afford to wait for bad weather."

"We're armed," Loomis pointed out.

Owenby snorted. "Those Red buggers travel in three- to six-lorry patrols most of the time, for protection. A breakdown out here could be fatal for a single lorry. Chances are there'll be more than a hundred well-armed troops. So we can't overpower the sods. Get that out of your head. If they sight us, we're done for. No papers, no right to be here, and a load of weapons and ammunition. No way to fight our way out of this one, Jack. You do follow me, don't you?"

Loomis nodded. He searched for alternatives. The road ran across a flat, treeless plain. Not a single bend or dip in either direction. And there was nothing to hide behind if trucks came into sight.

"We could go west about forty miles, where there's a bridge," Owenby said. "But our chances wouldn't be much better. We might as well chance it here."

"Break out a couple of the Kalashnikovs," Loomis said. "They'd give us a fighting chance."

"Not enough of one that you'd notice," Owenby said. "Besides, you can wager they'll have radios. So let's don't be stupid. Even if you wiped out a platoon by yourself, they'd have half the Red army pursuing you in a few hours."

"We could wait until sundown," Loomis said. "We'd be less noticeable in the changing light."

Reluctantly Owenby agreed. They pulled back and watched the road. Owenby spoke to the Gurkhas, and the yaks were turned loose to graze.

"If we're spotted, the buggers might mistake us for a band of *drokba* at this distance. If they're as lazy as I hope, they might not stop."

In midafternoon five trucks came along at a fast clip,

traveling west. They were moving almost bumper to bumper and did not slow. They were raising a faint spume of dust along the road and disappeared to the west.

"Maybe that's their patrol for today," Loomis said.

"Maybe. And maybe not. There seems to be no pattern. More could be along in ten minutes or not for two days."

"Any traffic on this road other than the army?" Loomis asked.

"Not to speak of. This isn't your ordinary bloody Gray Line tour. The Red buggers seldom issue permits to anyone for travel beyond Lhasa and Shigatse."

The sun sank lower. Long shadows distorted distances, images. Owenby ordered the yaks brought in close.

"Never thought I'd wish for a bloody sandstorm. But we can't wait. So there's no ducking it. We'd best be off."

Loomis walked to the yak carrying the rifle he had used in the pass. He reached into the pack and pulled it out.

"No!" Owenby shouted. "I told you no! Those are my bloody guns. And I say we don't fight, no matter what!"

After the battle in the pass, Loomis had taped two banana clips to the stock before returning the rifle to the baggage. He ripped a clip free, inserted it into the rifle, and worked the action to chamber a round.

"Do what you want," he told Owenby. "I don't intend to be taken."

Owenby stood facing him, legs spread, showing fight. "Don't be a bloody fool. If we're stopped, it'll be time for my game, not yours. There's always a chance I might be able to talk our way out of it."

"And if you can't?"

"One fact you've got to understand, Loomis. Those buggers are very good at what they do. You couldn't take down five or six lorries full of them on your best day."

"If it comes down to it, I can try."

"And if you could, then what? We're a week of travel from the border. And haven't you noticed? There's no bloody place to hide out here. They'd just get us sooner or later."

Loomis climbed into the saddle and held the rifle across his lap.

"We'd better move," he said. "There are no clouds. We won't have much twilight to work with."

Owenby hesitated, and for a moment Loomis thought he might protest further. But he jumped onto his yak and angrily lashed it into a trot, heading for the road.

"Fuck it," he shouted back to Loomis. "If the Red buggers stop us, probably won't make a bloody lot of difference what we do."

They hurried toward the road, constantly listening for the sound of distant motors. The western sky glowed red as the setting sun hit the dust of the upper atmosphere. Darkness seemed to seep from the ground, contrasting sharply with the pale light of the rising moon, growing ever brighter.

They reached the road and crossed it without stopping. On Owenby's order, one of the Gurkhas hurried back and eliminated their tracks with a whisk broom made from a handful of grass. Owenby hardly paused. They hurried on to the north.

They were less than three hundred yards from the road when they first heard the engines.

"Must be the same bloody bastards coming back," Owenby shouted. "And here we are with our asses hanging out like Piccadilly whores."

Lights came into view to the west. Owenby lashed his yak and broke into a trot. The Gurkhas pushed all of the animals into a run. But as the trucks grew near, Loomis left his saddle and ran forward to grab Owenby's reins, stopping him.

"Movement will attract attention," he said. "Let's stay perfectly still."

Owenby glanced up at the moon. "Too bright. They'll spot us, sure as shit."

But he shouted orders to the Gurkhas. They brought the string of yaks to a halt.

Loomis knelt, making less of a profile, and signaled for the others to get down. The Gurkhas eased behind the yaks, putting the animals between themselves and the road.

"I've never felt so bloody naked," Owenby said. "Are the buggers blind? How can they keep from seeing us?"

Loomis tried to imagine conditions in the trucks, with night coming on, darkness falling faster than the eye could adjust, and the moon and the truck lights providing additional complications. The soldiers would be tired after a long day's patrol. With luck, they might not notice a string of dark forms in the moonlight.

But the trucks slowed, then came to a brake-squealing halt a few yards short of where the yaks had crossed the road. Loomis brought his rifle up, ready.

The Red Chinese soldiers spilled out of the trucks and milled around the edge of the road. Loomis assumed they were searching for tracks. It was Owenby who first understood what they were doing.

"It's piss call," he whispered. "Don't shoot, Loomis! They've just stopped to take a bloody leak."

Still Loomis worried that one of the soldiers, while draining his bladder, might look out across the plain and become curious about those dark shadows out there in the moonlight.

Loomis hardly dared breathe, expecting at any moment a shout, an exploratory reconnaissance, or at least fingers of light probing into the darkness.

Long minutes passed. At last soldiers began climbing back into the trucks. A horn sounded, engines were started, and with the groan of gears the trucks pulled away. Soon they were increasing distance on their journey toward the east.

"I've aged ten bloody years in the last ten minutes," Owenby said. "Let's get the fuck away from this road."

They traveled by moonlight until well after midnight, and even then Owenby would not allow the Gurkhas to build a fire to warm their tea.

"We've come no more than thirty miles," he said. "A small fire can be seen farther than that in this country."

Through the remainder of the night Owenby was less than his usual effusive self. He seemed to be sulking. Loomis ignored him. The next morning, Owenby came out with what was bothering him.

"Loomis, I let you have your way in the pass because plainly that was your kind of game. Last night was different. I want you to understand right now that I'm in charge of this caravan. There can be no two ways about it. You do follow me, don't you?"

Loomis was irritated by his tone. "That's fine as long as I agree with you," he said. "If I don't, I'll do whatever I have to do."

Owenby had been harnessing his yak. He left the animal and came to stand in front of Loomis. "I don't think you understand what a narrow wicket that was last night. If you'd opened fire on those buggers, we'd be dead by now. I know this country. You don't. Believe me. There's always a chance I can talk our way out of a fix."

"And sometimes there may be a better chance of fighting our way out of it," Loomis told him. "If there is, I'll fight."

They stood for a time glaring at each other. The Gurkhas stood watching. They did not know the language, but they understood the situation.

"Put the rifle back in the pack," Owenby said.

The Kalashnikov still rode under Loomis's knee. He did not make a move toward it.

"Under the circumstances, I think I'd better keep it," he said.

Owenby studied him a long moment. "You're taking over the caravan. Is that it?"

"No," Loomis told him. "You know where we're going, how to get there. I'm only along for the ride. But you haven't leveled with me completely. I know that. So I'll keep the rifle. I'm just looking out for myself."

Again Owenby looked as if he might show fight. He

stood for a long moment in indecision. But he was unarmed, facing a loaded rifle.

"Then keep the bloody thing," he said. "Just remember that if you try to use it in the wrong situation, you'll get us all killed."

He returned to his yak and rode off.

They moved on, leaving the dispute unresolved. Owenby remained wrapped in an atypical silence.

In the early afternoon a dark mass appeared along the northern horizon. The Gurkhas became excited and talked animatedly among themselves, pointing.

"What is it?" Loomis asked Owenby.

"Bloody sandstorm, that's what. It'll make life miserable for a while. But we can forget about any pursuit. It'll wipe out all tracks."

The storm hit an hour later with gale-force winds. Owenby handed Loomis a pair of goggles. At first Loomis disdained their use. Soon he found them essential.

Visibility dropped to less than twenty yards. Still they rode on, buffeted constantly by the wind.

That night they did not try to raise the yak-hair tent. The Gurkhas made a lean-to shelter and they slept in the lee of that. They ate barley and yogurt, along with the inescapable grit.

The sandstorm lasted two days. On the third the sun rose into a clear sky. Owenby's good mood was restored.

"Today you'll see a marvelous sight," he promised.

In midmorning they came to an emerald lake surrounded by plains and high mountains. Loomis assumed it was one of the hundreds that dotted the map of the high plateau.

Bands of *drokba* were camped along the shore. Owenby turned toward the largest collection of black yak-hair tents. On the approach of the caravan, the people streamed out to greet them.

The men wore quilted wool knee-length coats or robes and factory-made boots. Although some wore caps, most had acquired wide-brimmed, Western-styled hats. The women wore colorful, patterned wool dresses and skirts, and an abundance of beaded necklaces, bracelets, and earrings.

Owenby moved among them, shaking hands, exchanging words of greeting. From the give-and-take of his conversations, Loomis gathered that Owenby's command of the language was limited but functional. He seemed to be well known and well liked among the *drokba.*

As Owenby, Loomis, and the Gurkhas made camp, the *drokba* returned to their work. Some of the women labored at the handles of the large churns used to make yogurt. A short distance from camp, men, women, and children returned to cutting, gathering, and binding grass to be stored as hay for the animals, to maintain them through the coming winter months.

The life of the *drokba* seemed idyllic. At sundown, herds of ewes, goats, and dris—female yaks—were brought in close to camp. Women swarmed out to milk them. There was much joking, shouting, and laughing among them.

Loomis and Owenby were invited into the tent of the *drokba* chief for a sumptuous supper. Afterward, filled with yogurt; *tsamba;* salted, buttered tea; and choice mutton, followed by a generous helping of Boodles gin, Owenby again grew talkative.

"Look at the buggers. You'd think they're barely eking out a living from this bloody land. But don't be fooled by appearances. Those yaks, sheep, and goats keep them in more than enough milk, butter, cheese, and yogurt. They sell the surplus to the hill tribes down south, or in the cities to the east. Those herds are also rich in hides and wool. A few years ago you couldn't give away one of those bloody goats out there, and now they're worth a fortune. Know why? They're cashmere goats. The price of cashmere has skyrocketed in the last few years. The *drokba* have always been well-to-do. Some of these lakes are the only source of salt for this part of Asia. They bag and sell salt all over Tibet, Nepal, Bhutan, northern India. These people may look like dirty peasants to you, old sod, but every family here probably could sell out and buy a neat bungalow on the Riviera."

As Owenby talked, it occurred to Loomis that Owenby was an even more slippery individual than Loomis had first assumed. Although he earlier had professed only a nodding acquaintance with the high plateau, plainly he had been here many times.

They lingered only overnight at the lake. The next morning they pushed on, still traveling northwest.

"How much farther?" Loomis asked.

Owenby laughed. "Bit weary, old sod? You can take heart. We're halfway there. Only another three hundred miles."

Loomis borrowed Owenby's map. As he studied the route they had come, the distance they yet had to go, there were questions that would not go away. Why would Buddhist monks summon him to this remote region? And what would they expect him to do?

4

Owenby dropped back to ride beside Loomis. "Today we should be there," he said.

Loomis did not answer. It seemed as if he had been riding across the high plateau forever. Since leaving the hut in the Himalayas they had come almost six hundred miles. And with every mile, the scenery was more spectacular.

Three days ago, they had crossed the second Chinese-built narrow dirt road, the one that ran across the middle of the plateau. Again they had taken a chance, but this time they had seen no vehicles. Owenby had said that this deep in the interior, washouts and landslides often kept the road closed for weeks at a time.

The trip had continued to be filled with assorted hardships. One afternoon they had endured a hailstorm that for thirty minutes pelted them with ice the size of a man's fist. The storm came up so suddenly that there had been no time to prepare. They could only huddle on the ground and endure the pounding. Loomis's back was still bruised and sore.

Now they were well to the north of the lakes and near the site for the rendezvous.

To the west the terrain stretched away perfectly flat for perhaps forty miles to a soaring range of mountains. To the northwest, no more than ten miles distant, another range jutted up from level ground. To the east and south lay others at varying distances. All were raw and unshaped, something like what the world must have been when it was new. Broken boulders, huge mounds of dirt were intermingled along the slopes, with no geological strata that Loomis could discern. Never had he seen such barren mountains anywhere in his travels about the earth.

The plains were hardly less spectacular. Throughout the six hundred miles not a tree, not a bush grew anywhere. Only a low, sparse grass.

Earlier in the day the sky had been clear, but now clouds were forming. Loomis looked ahead. Nothing broke the empty landscape except a faint, indistinct smudge on the horizon to the northwest.

As they rode, Loomis watched it for a time, thinking it might be a dust devil like those in open country back in Texas. But it seemed too dark for dust. After studying it for a while and finding no answer for his curiosity, he pointed.

"What's that on the horizon?"

Owenby squinted against the distance. He reached for his binoculars and trained them on the smudge for almost a full minute before replying.

"I haven't the foggiest, old sod. Too low for a cloud. Too dark for a grass fire."

He shouted to the Gurkhas. From their tones of reply, Loomis gathered that they also were mystified.

"We'll bloody well go see," Owenby said. "It's close to the agreed point of rendezvous."

They turned toward the smoke and quickened their pace. Yet more than two hours passed before Owenby would hazard a guess on what he saw through his binoculars.

"Looks like a *drokba* encampment that has burned. People are moving about. Maybe it was an accident. Maybe not. You'd best break out your Kalashnikov, old sod. This may be in your department."

He handed the binoculars to Loomis. He studied the figures moving around the burned area. From the distance, he could not determine whether they were in uniform.

"Could it be the Red Chinese?" he asked.

"Not bloody likely. They don't venture this far away from the roads without lorries or equipment of some kind."

Within another hour they were close enough to confirm that it was a burned encampment. Thirty or more bodies were lying to one side in neat rows. The natives about the camp were so busy they did not notice the approach of the caravan. But suddenly someone yelled, and many of the nomads fled across the plain on foot.

"The beggars," Owenby said. He stood in his stirrups, cupped his hands around his mouth, and shouted. Several of the running figures stopped. Owenby shouted again, adding his name. The natives started returning to the encampment.

"You can put the bloody rifle away," he said to Loomis. "Poor devils are scared enough."

Loomis felt he should keep it handy. He compromised by again tucking it under his leg, out of sight.

All the tents of the encampment were but charred rubble, with the contents still smoldering. Some of the people were on their knees beside the dead, foreheads to the ground, praying. Occasionally a wail of grief rose among them. Among the thirty or more dead were men, women, and children. From the bloodstains on their clothing, Loomis assumed that all had been shot.

Several of the nomads came toward them, shouting to Owenby. Owenby left his yak and went forward to talk with them. He motioned for Loomis to join him.

Loomis returned the rifle to its pack and walked over

to where Owenby was talking with the natives. Again Owenby seemed worried.

"I'm not sure what to think. They say Lhalde arrived here two days ago and pitched his tent right over there."

He pointed to a black spot on the ground. The dry grass had been burned for some distance around it.

"These buggers say that yesterday afternoon late, about a dozen men came riding up on horses, waving guns. They shot up the camp, killing everyone who couldn't get away in time. Some of these people were out with the herds and saw what happened. They say the same men took Lhalde away, along with the three monks who were with him."

"Chinese?"

"Turks, these buggers think. They believe they were Uighurs from up north. But they're not for damned sure."

Loomis walked over and looked at the place where Lhalde's tent had been pitched. All of the equipment in it had been burned. Empty brass cartridges littered the ground. Loomis picked up a few. All were from 7mm cartridges. He examined tracks, but found too many to evaluate.

It occurred to him that perhaps more parts of the mystery were falling into place. The ambush in the pass had been set by a Turk. Maybe it and Lhalde's kidnapping were connected.

But he needed more information, and Owenby was still holding out on him. He walked back to where Owenby was talking with the nomads.

"Who was to take delivery of the guns?" he asked. "Lhalde?"

"That's my business," Owenby said.

"And now it's mine. Murder and kidnapping fall in my department. So let's have some straight answers for a change. What about the other merchandise? Was it all for Lhalde?"

Owenby hesitated, and for a moment Loomis thought

he would refuse to cooperate. But he gave a shrug of resignation.

"What the fuck. It probably makes no difference now. Yes, my friend. All was for Lhalde. This whole bloody trip was for Lhalde. The guns, the goods, you."

"You've made trips for him before?"

Again Owenby hesitated. "A few."

"How many?"

Owenby sighed. "A dozen, maybe. Look, up to now it was a simple game, smuggling ordinary goods past the Chinese. Lhalde used me because he could trust me to take precautions about the location of the lamasery."

"What kind of goods?" Loomis insisted.

"Manufactured stuff, mostly. You see, his lamasery is supplied with most of their needs by loyal *drokba.* Or they make their own. But two or three times a year they need other things. Needles. Scissors. Reference books. Pots and pans. I purchased the bloody stuff and smuggled it in to him."

"Where did you bring it? Here?"

"Wherever he said. He always set the rendezvous, the time and place. The idea was to be extra careful so no one could trail him back to the lamasery. His loyal *drokba* made sure, driving herds of sheep and goats over his tracks."

"He ever order guns before?"

"Never. And it was quite a bloody surprise, I'll tell you. But he has his connections. He knows I've dealt in guns. And he trusts me. So he just added them to the list."

"He specify Kalashnikovs?"

"No. He only asked for good modern weapons and ammunition. The Kalashnikovs were the best I could find on such short notice."

Loomis considered the possibilities. Plainly Lhalde must have known about some threat to his safety, or to that of the lamasery. So he had ordered the guns.

But Buddhists are pacifists. So perhaps Lhalde had

arranged for a mercenary—Loomis—to come in and put the guns to use.

Loomis found one basic flaw in that line of reasoning: Surely Lhalde could have found good fighting men much closer, without sending halfway around the world for one.

And how could solving such a basic security problem be "of lasting benefit . . . to many oppressed people, and perhaps to all mankind"?

Clearly major parts of the mystery were still missing.

Loomis circled the campsite, seeking clues. He found none. He knew he was out of his element in this country.

"Herdsmen usually are good trackers," he said to Owenby. "Ask them if there's anyone among them who's an expert."

Owenby talked for a time with a group. After much discussion, one man was singled out. He was square built and wore his hair in pigtails. As with so many of the natives, his eyes were mere slits, perhaps from constantly staring over long distances. He wore a blanket looped over one shoulder and a black leather cap that had seen better days.

"This is Gentun," Owenby told Loomis. "They say he can track a kid goat across a solid rock mountain. He says he'll help us. His brother, sister-in-law, and four nieces and nephews were killed by the bloody buggers."

"Hire him," Loomis said. "And tell your men to unpack two or three of those Kalashnikovs and some ammunition. If you're game, we'll see what we can do about getting Lhalde back."

Owenby planted himself in front of Loomis with feet spread in what Loomis had come to recognize as his stance of belligerence. "Just a jolly minute, my good man. As you said, kidnapping and murder are in your department. I only agreed to deliver the goods and you to this rendezvous. Nothing more. I can't help it if the man isn't here."

"And I only agreed to come here to listen to Lhalde's

proposition," Loomis said. "So far I haven't heard it. Someone seems determined to keep me from hearing it. I didn't travel halfway around the world just to quit and remain curious the rest of my life. I'm going to find Lhalde and listen to what he has to say."

Again Owenby hesitated a long moment. "All right, old chum. I'll supply you with two guns. And two yaks. That's all I can do."

"You can come with me and help me with the language," Loomis told him. "I don't see how you can do any less and look yourself in the mirror."

"No," Owenby said. "You're on your own on this, my friend."

"I thought you said you and Lhalde go way back, to the time you were his financial adviser. I thought you said he trusted you, believed in you enough to continue your association after your fall from grace."

Owenby glanced toward the west, in the direction the kidnappers had gone, and avoided Loomis's eyes. "Loyalty's one thing, old sod. Getting shot's another. Every man has his limitations."

"You never know what your limits are until you try them," Loomis told him. "What'll you do with the rest of those guns out here in Buddhist country? Sell some more of them to Lhalde's enemies?"

Owenby glanced back to where the Gurkhas were stacking the packs. For a time he seemed lost in thought. "You're right about one bloody fact. Most of my working capital is tied up in those goddamned guns. With the money from them, and for delivering you, I stood to leave this godforsaken country with enough for a stake to try to buy my way back into the world."

"Maybe you still can," Loomis said. "Those Turks have a twenty-four-hour head start on us. But they won't be expecting pursuit. If they had intended to kill Lhalde, they'd have done it here. I'd say we'd have a good chance of getting him back. But both of us would have a hell of a lot better chance than one."

Owenby's further hesitation was brief. "All right," he said after a moment. "I'll go. But don't expect any heroics out of me. I'm just not the type."

After four hours of steady travel, the tracker Gentun suddenly reined in his yak and waited for Loomis and Owenby to catch up. He spoke a phrase to Owenby and pointed.

"He says they stopped here last night," Owenby told Loomis. "And they buried something over there."

The two low piles of rocks blended into the terrain so well that Loomis might have missed them. He slid off his mount, walked over to the first pile of stones, and began uncovering the mound.

After he had removed fewer than a dozen rocks, a hand came into view. On first glance, Loomis felt his anger mounting. Where fingernails should have been, there was only crusted blood. Loomis knew he should expect nothing less from bandits who would shoot down men, women, and children in cold blood. Yet somehow the small, uncalloused hand without fingernails was even more atrocious.

Owenby came to help with the rocks. Within minutes they had the body uncovered.

Loomis examined it carefully. The face was that of a youth, perhaps no more than nineteen or twenty. The nose was broken. The teeth were shattered, and the eyeballs appeared to have been burned out with hot irons. Loomis opened the robe and pulled the underclothing aside. Burns covered the chest. The penis and testicles had been burned away.

"One of the monks," Owenby said. He caught Loomis's quizzical glance. "Monks wear ankle-length robes like that. Other male Tibetans wear them calf-length. This must have been one of Lhalde's assistants."

The other mound contained the body of another young monk. It was in even worse shape. Both kneecaps had been crushed into splinters.

"The buggers must be trying to extract information on

the location of the lamasery," Owenby mused. "Obviously these two didn't tell. At least, not until too late for themselves."

The tracker Gentun was circling around the campsite, studying tracks.

"Let's get going," Loomis said.

They put the stones back over the bodies and went on. A short time later the sun disappeared over a distant mountain range. Darkness came abruptly. Although the temperature dropped to near zero, they did not build a fire.

After they had eaten cold mutton and yogurt, Gentun spoke to Owenby.

"He says if we have some money, he thinks he can get us fresh mounts at a camp not far from here. What do you think? This could be a gambit for him to run out on us."

Loomis considered the risks. They had ridden the animals hard all day. Fresh mounts would give them great advantage. And Gentun had been dependable thus far.

"It's worth a try," he said.

Gentun took three gold coins from Loomis and disappeared into the night. Loomis and Owenby curled up in their blankets and slept. Shortly after midnight, Gentun returned. He had purchased three yaks. He said they were superior to most in the region.

At three in the morning the moon rose, giving them enough light to go on, but for a while their pace was slowed. Often, especially on rocky terrain, Gentun dismounted and walked. Twice he lost the track and they moved in widening circles until he picked it up again.

But with daylight, Gentun resumed the fast trot he had maintained most of thirty-six hours.

In late morning they came to the place where the Turks had spent the second night. There they found another mutilated body, covered with dirt. They dug it out, examined it, reburied it, and went on.

As they rode on westward, Loomis began to plan

ahead. Gentun had said the Uighurs were not traveling fast because their horses were not accustomed to the altitude. With the Turks also spending considerable time at their nightly sport, torturing monks, they might be able to catch up with them soon. And the country was so flat that any movement could be seen for miles.

He called to Owenby. "Tell Gentun to keep a sharp lookout. We don't want them to see us first."

Owenby and Gentun talked for a time in Tibetan.

"He says the shit from their horses is now about four or five hours old," Owenby said. "It never occurred to me to wonder."

"Ask him if he has any idea where they could be headed," Loomis said.

Owenby asked the question and Gentun pointed.

"He thinks they're aiming for the base of those mountains. An old caravan trail runs past there, toward the north, into Xinjiang and Turk country."

Loomis briefly considered cutting across, perhaps setting up his own trap. But after a moment of reflection he rejected the idea. The country was too flat. He was not likely to find a good site for an ambush.

Hours later, in midafternoon, Gentun again spoke to Owenby and pointed.

"Old sod, we've caught up with them," Owenby said. "Look straight ahead. That black speck between here and those mountains. Gentun says that's them."

Loomis stood in his stirrups and shaded his eyes. He could barely make out a minuscule dot on the vast, barren landscape. He would never have noticed it from this distance. But these *drokba* were accustomed to living in such immense space. Loomis drew rein. Perhaps someone among the Turks also was capable of glancing back and seeing three men following on yaks.

Owenby and Gentun also had stopped. They sat in their saddles, looking at Loomis.

"What now?" Owenby asked.

"Hang back out of sight and wait for darkness, I guess," Loomis said.

"And what then?"

"We'll go in and see if we can separate Lhalde from the Turks."

Owenby eyed the distant dot. "My dear boy, I told you, by training and inclination I'm basically a banker. Shooting people is foreign to my nature."

"Don't you know how to fire those guns you've been peddling?"

"Only as a salesman demonstrating his wares, old sod. I've never killed anyone."

"You'll get the hang of it," Loomis said. "What about Gentun? Will he go in with us?"

Owenby and the tracker conversed in Tibetan for several minutes. Owenby shook his head.

"He says he'll guide you in. But he won't use a gun. He's a Buddhist, and Buddhists won't kill. Not even a fly, much less a man."

"Not even in self-defense?"

"Not under any circumstances. Loomis, old sod, you've got to understand these people if you plan to work with them. In India some Buddhists wear gauze over their nostrils so they won't inadvertently breathe in a gnat. They carry brooms to sweep the ground in front of them so they won't accidentally step on an insect. Tibetans aren't quite that fanatic. But few will kill their own meat. They call in those who practice the trade to butcher their sheep. It has to do with reincarnation, karma. They believe you carry all the bad crap from each life over into the next and you're judged accordingly."

"Then it'll be you and me," Loomis said.

Owenby frowned. "Loomis, I told you. I won't go in with you. I'm just not cut out for this sort of thing."

"It'll be easy," Loomis said. "We'll go up on them in the dark. Just put the selector on automatic, put the sights on a man's chest, and squeeze. A short burst. No more than three or four rounds. Shift targets. You'll only have to be careful you don't hit Lhalde."

"While those buggers shoot back," Owenby said. "Believe me, old sod. You'll be better off alone. To tell the truth, I don't know how I'd react if bullets started coming my way. I'm sure I'd be quite erratic."

Loomis appreciated the frankness. But he badly needed the extra firepower, for diversionary purposes, if nothing else.

"You'll be so busy you won't have time to think," Loomis promised. "You've stood up to me. Why not them? I'm sure you'll do fine."

Owenby grimly shook his head. "Loomis, this isn't a momentary consideration. My father was a brigadier in the big one. I'm descended from a long line of military people. My mother grew up as the daughter of the regiment her father commanded. My older brother did her quite proud. Royal Military College at Sandhurst, rapid rise to half colonel before a land mine blew off his legs at Belfast. Off at the hips. We buried him in pieces. So you see, I'm the black sheep. No flags, guns, and glory for me, thank you. I've spent my life avoiding my so-called duty. Thank you, but no thank you."

Loomis was remembering Owenby's wide-legged, obstinate stance and frequent bursts of belligerence. He felt that Owenby was selling himself short.

"What about Lhalde, your deal with him?" Loomis asked. "Don't you feel a sense of obligation to him?"

Owenby did not answer.

"I only need you for backup," Loomis went on. "Just to fire a few rounds, keep them confused, make them think there's more of us."

Owenby remained silent for a time. Loomis did not pressure him further. At last Owenby seemed to come to a hard decision.

"All right. I'll go with you. But bear in mind it's all new to me."

Again they ate cold food, finishing all they had brought with them. Afterward, while they waited for darkness, Loomis quizzed Gentun, with Owenby serving as interpreter.

As Loomis suspected, Gentun had assembled a great deal of information from small clues.

"He thinks there are eight Turks," Owenby translated. "He believes Lhalde is the only monk left alive. All of this he has gathered from the way the riders guide their mounts, a stray footprint here and there. I wouldn't put too much stock in it."

But Loomis did. He had worked with good trackers before.

Again darkness quickly followed sunset. The temperature dropped. Loomis readied a Kalashnikov and tied three banana clips under his coat. He made a Mexican poncho out of his blanket and strapped his belt over it.

He then showed Owenby how to carry extra clips for quick insertion and coached him on the tricks of maintaining control of the weapon on full automatic, keeping it on target.

While they made preparations, a faint pinpoint of light glimmered in the distance.

"They've built a big fire," Owenby said. "I'd guess they're heating the irons to play games with Lhalde."

With the arrival of solid darkness, they began the long walk toward the Turk camp. The ground was covered with rough stones, making progress difficult and noisy.

Yet so great was the distance that after an hour the camp hardly seemed closer. Gentun stopped and whispered to Owenby.

"This is as far as he goes," Owenby said. "He says he has a wife and six children, and must think of them." Owenby laughed. "Hell, I may have six children, too, somewhere. I've never bothered to ask."

Loomis and Owenby continued their approach, with Loomis leading the way. After a time he dropped to a hunter's crouch, even though he doubted they could be seen from the camp.

Gradually details around the camp began to grow clear. Men in long sheepskin robes milled around the fire. A low black tent stood a few yards beyond. Horses were tethered off to the left. Packs and baggage were piled beside the tent.

Only three men carried rifles. Loomis assumed that

they had been assigned to sentry duty, although they did not appear alert. Not one spent any time searching the darkness around them. Loomis knew that the fire would tend to destroy their night vision.

Four or five rifles were stacked by the swivels in front of the tent. Loomis counted six men in the light of the fire. Unless Gentun had been wrong in his count, two were nowhere in sight.

Growing wary, Loomis lay on the ground and waited. He signaled for Owenby to do the same.

Ten minutes or more passed. Then a tent flap moved. The other two men emerged. They were dragging a tall, gray-haired man.

A camp stool was set up in front of the fire. The elderly man was taken to it and forced to sit. Despite the freezing temperature, he was naked to the waist.

Owenby crawled closer. "That's Lhalde," he whispered.

"We'll move up another twenty or thirty yards," Loomis whispered back. "When the shooting starts, you take the two on the right. Stay behind me. I'll signal when it's time."

He started the long crawl. The ground was covered with stones that cut into his knees and elbows. He moved cautiously, keeping low, pausing occasionally to watch the Turks.

A big man in a large fur hat was directing operations. He stood over Lhalde and shouted. From the inflections, Loomis assumed he was asking questions, demanding answers. Growing impatient, the man began punctuating his questions with blows from a leather strap. Even from the distance of two hundred yards, the slaps of leather on flesh were surprisingly loud.

A white-hot iron was brought from the fire. The big man thrust it close to Lhalde's face. Lhalde did not flinch.

Apparently an interpreter was being used, for now Loomis could hear the big man's questions repeated with less volume and in another tongue. Soon all attention was focused on the drama beside the fire. Loomis took advantage of the diversion to crawl closer.

But abruptly the big man lost his composure. He shouted angrily, then hit Lhalde harder, knocking him off the stool. When two Turks returned Lhalde to his seat, blood covered his mouth and face.

The big man shouted more orders. Another hot iron was brought. The tip was placed on Lhalde's bare chest. Slowly it was drawn across Lhalde's ribs. Lhalde stiffened, but did not make a sound.

Loomis raised his rifle and pushed the selector from safe to automatic. But the angle was wrong. The big man had taken a step to the right, placing himself partially between Loomis and Lhalde. Loomis could not fire, for the bullet might pass through and strike Lhalde.

Loomis turned and raised a fist to Owenby, who nodded that he was ready. Loomis was surprised how plainly he could see Owenby's face in the light of the distant fire.

Again he raised his rifle. More questions were being shouted at Lhalde, who still remained silent. The big man gestured, and another hot iron was brought to him from the fire.

He took a short step to the left to receive it, giving Loomis his chance. He narrowed his sights to a head shot and squeezed the trigger.

The gun fired. The big man dropped, his head spewing a red fog over the camp fire.

For an instant the tableau in the camp remained frozen. Then Owenby's gun sounded in a long burst. The two men on the right fell.

Loomis shot the two on the left. As he expected, the three remaining Turks ran to the side of the tent where the rifles were stacked. Firing short individual bursts, Loomis cut them down.

He jammed another clip into his rifle and rose to his feet.

Lhalde had fallen off the stool. Around the campfire, nothing moved.

Holding his rifle at ready, Loomis cautiously walked into the camp. He glanced at each body, then kicked the old Mausers to one side.

Lhalde lay on his back. His hands were tied behind him. An ugly Arabic inscription was burned deep into his chest. As Loomis leaned over him, Lhalde looked up and smiled with bloody lips. He spoke in English with a slight BBC accent.

"Mr. Loomis, I presume. I'm gratified to see that you've already started on your difficult and dangerous task."

Loomis cut the rawhide from Lhalde's wrists.

"I wouldn't know," he said. "I haven't yet been told what I'm expected to do."

Lhalde sat up and pulled his robe closed, covering his bare chest and the inscription on it. Loomis was impressed with the old man's dignity, especially under the circumstances. Badly beaten and burned, he undoubtedly was in considerable pain. But he gave no sign. He rose to his feet, folded each arm into the opposite sleeve of his robe, and spoke as calmly as if he were receiving Loomis admidst the peaceful surroundings of his monastery instead of in a Turk camp with bodies littering the ground around him.

"Perhaps I should have been more forthcoming in my correspondence with you, Mr. Loomis, and informed you more fully of what the task entails," he said. "But I assure you that deficiency can now be quickly remedied."

5

The hour was late. Loomis and Lhalde sat in the low black goat-hair tent of the Uighurs. The interior was only faintly illuminated by a small yak-butter lamp. Owenby and Gentun were outside, digging a shallow grave for the eight bodies.

Earlier, Lhalde's wounds had been tended and they all had feasted on the captured Uighur provisions. Gentun had brewed a pot of the salted, buttered tea that apparently was the Tibetan national drink. Now Lhalde sat in a relaxed lotus position on a thick sheepskin, savoring the last of his tea. Although his wounds must be painful, Loomis had yet to see him give any sign.

"You must understand that in asking you to come here we surrendered to the demands of our desperate straits," Lhalde said softly. "Normally we wouldn't even consider resorting to violence as the solution to *any* difficulty."

Loomis acknowledged the point with a nod. He was still studying Lhalde, who bore the obvious stamp of an exceptional man. His Oriental features were subdued, his skin light. His gray hair was straight and combed straight back, parted slightly in the middle. He was in his late seventies or early eighties, and there was no mistaking the intelligence in his dark, smoky eyes. In a proper three-piece suit, Lhalde easily could be mistaken for a distinguished banker or barrister in the clubs around London.

"In fact," Lhalde went on, "it was your demonstrated reluctance toward violence that first led us to you. Many of our sources of information mentioned that you never kill unless you consider it absolutely necessary. But we also were told that when you must kill you do not hesitate. I believe this combination will serve us well in the present circumstances."

Again Loomis remained silent. He wondered how Lhalde had managed to conduct such a thorough investigation without at least some word getting back to him. Lhalde must indeed possess a tight, elaborate network of sources.

"We also were attracted to your sense of compassion and fair play," Lhalde said. "We were informed of many instances in which you allowed a defeated enemy to live. We also noted your preference for the side of the righteous and for what I believe you Americans term the underdog."

Lhalde paused and sipped the last of his tea. He frowned, as if searching for words.

"Lastly, and perhaps most importantly, we came to know of your strong marital ties and of your obvious commitment to your work that so often takes you away from home."

Loomis felt that bit of snooping went too far. It was too personal. He opened his mouth to protest. Lhalde raised a hand, palm outward.

"Please, it was necessary that this be said. You must understand that we're not just hiring a mercenary to perform a service. We chose *you.* And we chose you with great care. Your recognition of this fact is fundamental to our working arrangement."

Loomis closed his mouth and waited.

"Owenby said he has described to you our political

situation in Tibet. So I won't go back over that ground. But it's necessary that you know something about us in order to understand our present difficulty."

Loomis nodded to acknowledge the point.

"Our order of monks is one of the oldest in existence in the world today. We first came into this region from India in the seventh century. Fourteen hundred years ago. We came over the Silk Road and brought Buddhism to the Far East. On few instances in the course of human events has the dissemination of a religion been more successful. We, and a few more like us, spread Buddhism throughout China and Japan. We even converted most of the warlords of that day to our way of thinking."

Loomis was intrigued by Lhalde's use of "we." Lhalde spoke as if he himself had been there.

"Then, in the thirteenth and fourteenth centuries, another harsher, more militant religion came over the Silk Road. The Islamic faith. A *jihad*—or holy war—was declared against Buddhists. Thousands of peaceful Buddhists were slaughtered. Those were terrible times. Wars of religion ruled this region through the next two centuries. The struggles were complex, and I won't attempt to recount them except to say that our order fled into what is now south-central Tibet. There, isolated from the world, we performed our work unmolested until the beginning of the second half of the century we are in now."

Loomis felt a tingling along his scalp. Lhalde talked of centuries as if they were days and implied that he had lived through them.

"The invasion of Tibet by Red China in nineteen fifty and the Cultural Revolution of nineteen fifty-nine were the worst disasters our order has suffered in all our fourteen hundred years," Lhalde continued. "Or perhaps I should say the worst until now."

He paused. Loomis waited without comment.

"When our lamasery outside Lhasa was bombed and destroyed in nineteen fifty-nine, we loaded our treasures and fled deep into the high plateau. Over a period of years, with the help of loyal *drokba,* we dug caves in a mountain some distance from here. There we have rededicated our lamasery and gone on with our work."

Again Lhalde paused. He shifted his weight on the sheepskin, perhaps in deference to his wounds.

"The Xinjiang Province to our north has remained predominately Muslim since that religion came into the region in the thirteenth century. Recently, militant elements among them have vowed to renew the *jihad,* or holy war. It has come to us from several sources that these militants now have sworn to destroy all Buddhists remaining in Tibet, and most especially the Kamala Lama and our lamasery. We are the principal target because the Kamala Lama is perhaps the most revered and important of the lamas still residing in Tibet." Lhalde gestured to the door of the tent. "Those Uighurs you killed tonight are members of the militant group sworn to renew the *jihad.*"

Loomis thought of the broken and mutilated bodies of the young monks. "So they tortured you, and your monks, trying to make you reveal the location of the lamasery?"

Lhalde nodded affirmatively. "My brave, courageous young assistants wouldn't tell them, and died with their lips sealed. But of course we of our order are aware that in time the Muslims will learn our secret. It's inevitable. I doubt all our followers can endure what my assistants suffered. Not without telling the Uighurs whatever they wish to know."

Loomis was mildly disappointed. The "difficult and dangerous" task that "might benefit all mankind" now seemed no more than a routine security problem. Apparently he had come all this way to guard a monastery.

"The Chinese and the Uighurs are like the Vandals who swarmed down on ancient Rome," Lhalde went on. "They only know how to destroy. It's true that in nineteen eighty China reversed itself and decreed that the practice of religion again would be allowed. But the Lhasa uprising of nineteen eighty-nine brought renewed repressions. Thus far, no lamaseries in this country have returned to open society. Most have fled into exile in India or Nepal. We are one of the very few remaining in Tibet and still in existence."

Lhalde fell silent. For a time he seemed lost in thought. Gently, Loomis prodded.

"So you want the Kamala Lama and the lamasery protected. How many men do you have who might use weapons?"

Lhalde considered his answer carefully. "About fifty. They are our warrior monks. They have dedicated their lives to the protection of our lama."

"What about their karma? Will they kill?"

Lhalde hesitated. "If absolutely necessary. You see, they've accepted the karma of killing as a sacrifice to be made in this life for their lama."

Loomis doubted he would receive much help from fifty reluctant warriors. Prospects for the safety of the monastery did not appear good. Thirty rifles and fifty men would be woefully inadequate if the Uighurs came in any force at all. He had just seen graphic examples of their viciousness. He felt he should begin now to lay the groundwork for turning down the job.

"Understand, I'd have to take a look at the lay of the land around the lamasery before I could judge whether it's defensible."

"Of course," Lhalde said. "But there are other aspects for you to consider."

He paused, as if evaluating how much to reveal.

"As I told you, our order came into this region from India in the seventh century. Through the years many trips were made back and forth over the Himalayas, and through the mountain passes of what is now Kashmir and Afghanistan. We traveled those thousands of miles often, always in search of knowledge. Over the centuries we gathered and brought into Tibet a wealth of sacred writings in Sanskrit, Pali, Vedic, Hebrew, Latin, other languages. In more recent centuries we have translated and preserved those manuscripts. Meanwhile, down through all those centuries, as the result of warfare and religious persecutions, many of those same texts now have been lost elsewhere. Consequently, they survive only in Tibet and only in our lamasery."

He leaned toward Loomis and lowered his voice to just above a whisper.

"Today our lamasery is the richest repository of ancient writings in the world. We are the custodians of some of the earliest and most valuable books mankind possesses. We have preserved canonical scriptures containing the direct words of the Gautama Buddha, dating back to the fourth century B.C. These sacred scriptures have been lost to Pali, Sanskrit, Chinese, all other languages. We also possess early texts of the Old Testament—the Septuagint—now lost to Jewish scholars for more than a thousand years. We retain the oldest versions of many books of the New Testament, including portions of the so-called Q document containing many direct quotations from Jesus Christ expurgated at the earliest church councils and now unknown to modern Christian scholars. These writings are beyond price." He pounded the sheepskin with a long bony forefinger. *"They must not be destroyed!"*

Loomis felt a shiver run up his spine. This importance was more what he had hoped the "task" might entail.

"How far is it from here to the lamasery?" he asked.

"A little more than a hundred miles, west by southwest."

"And how many monks do you have altogether?"

"About three hundred and fifty. Some live outside the lamasery, among the *drokba* who tend the flocks that provide our needs." He met Loomis's gaze. "Mr. Loomis, as I said in the letter, if you'll perform this holy mission for us, we're prepared to pay double your usual fee."

Loomis carefully considered his personal situation. He had told Maria Elena he most likely would be away from telephones six weeks or more. If he accepted the job, his absence might be even longer and last well beyond the end of her location shoot in Spain. He really wanted in the worst way to be home when she returned.

But he was tired of mundane jobs, dealing with governments, revolutionaries, and corporations. This job promised to be refreshingly different. And with the rare manuscripts at stake, it truly might be one that would make a difference, have a lasting effect on the world.

"I'll be happy to see what I can do to help," he said.

He and Lhalde shook hands. At that moment Owenby and Gentun came back into the tent.

"We planted the buggers," Owenby said. "Not very deep. But they should stay under until the next sandstorm." He glanced at Loomis and Lhalde. "I gather you two have concluded your deal."

"I've promised to see what I can do," Loomis said. "My first concern is the shortage of weapons. Thirty won't be nearly enough."

"Some of the *drokba* have weapons," Lhalde said.

Owenby snickered. He went to the smoldering fire and helped himself to tea.

"Flintlocks, mostly," he said. "Along with a few matchlocks. Aside from what the Uighurs and Red buggers are carrying, and the thirty rifles I just smuggled in, there probably isn't another twentieth-century weapon in all of western Tibet."

"Matchlocks?" Loomis asked. He had never seen one outside a museum.

"Some of the *drokba* use them for hunting," Owenby said. "I've seen quite a few in this region."

"Is there any chance at all of buying more guns?" Loomis asked Owenby.

"Not this side of Kathmandu. I could go there, buy whatever's available, and bring them back. But with three or four weeks' travel each way, I might arrive too late for whatever purpose you have in mind."

Loomis nodded agreement. The point was well taken. With the ambush in the pass and the kidnapping of Lhalde, clearly the Uighurs already were actively engaged in their *jihad.* He might not have much time to prepare.

"I'm committed to helping the monks," Loomis said to Owenby. "What about you?"

Owenby's glance went to Loomis, then to Lhalde, and back to Loomis. "What do you mean, what about me? I delivered the goods. I'm ready to return to Kathmandu. That's what about me."

"If I take this job, I'll need someone beside me who speaks the language," Loomis explained. "In short, I'll need an assistant."

Owenby waved a hand and shook his head vehemently. "Oh, no! Oh, no! Remember? That's your profession, old sod, not mine."

"You did well out there tonight," Loomis told him. "Maybe you were born for it."

"That little exercise was too easy," Owenby said. "Nobody was shooting back."

"Mr. Owenby, your assistance in this matter would be invaluable to us," Lhalde said. "We would be prepared to reward you very well."

Owenby looked at him for a moment. "How well?"

Lhalde used Tibetan monetary terms meaningless to Loomis.

Owenby's eyes widened. He looked at Loomis.

"That's tempting. But the fact is that money would do me no good whatsoever if I'm dead. You've seen what those sods can do."

"We'll go examine the monastery. If the odds appear too great, we'll recommend exile. I promise."

Owenby hesitated, then shook his head. "I'm simply not your man. I have animals and equipment to consider, not to mention business commitments back in Kathmandu. Besides, my Gurkhas expect me to take them home. They want no part in this war."

Loomis thought ahead to the difficulty of the language barrier. Lhalde said he was the only person at the lamasery who spoke English, except for the Kamala Lama. Lhalde was an old man, with other duties to perform. Loomis could hardly expect him to put in long days drilling troops. Owenby was the only answer.

"Your Gurkhas could take care of your animals and equipment," Loomis pointed out. "They know the way back to Kathmandu. They could fulfill your business commitments."

"Not as well as I," Owenby insisted. "I must be there."

Loomis tried a new tack. "You've mentioned you'd like to buy your way back into the world. Wouldn't this help you?"

Owenby did not answer for a moment. He sighed deeply.

"Loomis, you have a way of hitting a fellow where he lives. It's true. I've been told that with restitution of the missing funds the bank will drop all charges. If I could gather enough cash to play the beans again, and score big, my troubles would be over. Even the bonding company will let bygones be bygones, if the money's right. Money respects money. Sometime, old sod, I positively must tell you my theory of how money chases money, in a life all its own, exclusive of the hopes and desires of we mere mortals."

"Then this could be your way out," Loomis said quietly. "And what's your alternative? You want to be a border trader and smuggler the rest of your life?"

Owenby winced. "See? You indeed have a way of going for the jugular." He hesitated. When he again spoke, his voice was softer, his tone more thoughtful. "I brought my mother out to Hong Kong a few years back. I believe I almost convinced her there's glory enough in the world aside from flag and regiment. Could be that's why I overreached, attempting to drive home my argument." Again he hesitated. "Now my stories are wearing thin, of how I'm on holiday or straightening out the affairs of a branch bank. It *would* be marvelously nice to step out from behind all the sham." He met Loomis's gaze. "All right, old sod. We'll give it a try."

With the matter settled, Loomis was eager to get moving. Yet further delay was inevitable. He and

Owenby must return to the site of the *drokba* massacre, pick up the rest of the guns, and release Owenby's Gurkhas to return to their homes in Kathmandu.

Four or five days would be lost. And already other Uighurs might be on Lhalde's back trail, trying to follow it to the caves.

"How soon will you be ready to travel?" he asked Lhalde.

Lhalde did not hesitate. "I'm ready now. From talk I overheard in this camp, I gather there are other Uighurs near. They were expected to join this group tomorrow or the next day."

"How many?" Loomis asked.

"I don't know," Lhalde replied. "They didn't say."

6

The Tibetan was brought into camp in a rope basket strung between two horses. The laughter and shouting brought Turhan Oztrak out of his tent. He stood under the canopy and watched impassively as his men dragged the captive along the ground at a dead run and bounced him through the campfire, sending embers flying.

Oztrak was mildly irritated by the foolish play. But he did not stop it.

Sevki Erek came toward him laughing, looking back at the fun. Erek was covered with grime from many days of hard riding. He genuflected to Oztrak. Then they embraced.

Oztrak carefully kept his emotions in check. He was immensely relieved that Erek had returned from his dangerous expedition into Tibet. But as commander of the *jihad,* Oztrak constantly was forced to set his personal feelings aside.

Erek gestured toward the captive. "He is only an imbecile. Truly, an idiot. We brought him back, my commander, only because we thought he might possess useful information somewhere in his small brain."

Oztrak fixed Erek with a hard stare. "Your prisoner hasn't yet been interrogated?"

Erek shrugged. "I tried, my commander. But I could make no sense of his rantings. Gungor took our interpreter with him when he went after Lhalde."

From below, a resounding cheer erupted as the *drokba* again was bounced through the fire.

"Then go stop that foolishness this instant," Oztrak ordered. "If they kill him before he is interrogated, it could be a lost opportunity."

"Yes, my commander," Erek said. "It will be done."

Erek walked to the edge of the drill field and shouted to his lieutenants. Oztrak stood admiring the youth's stiff military bearing, his imposing presence. Despite his comparative inexperience, Oztrak had selected him early for high command. He was intelligent and a hard worker. With his full black beard and moustache, sparkling eyes, and handsome features, he was all Oztrak would have wished his oldest son to be, if his son had lived through the fighting in Afghanistan. Although Erek was a Kazakh, not a Uighur, he was a dedicated Muslim and totally devoted to the *jihad.*

Oztrak only regretted he would not take his duties more seriously. He too often was involved with women and other mindless entertainments. And too frequently he did not consider the full consequences of his actions, such as allowing his men this fun with the captive. But Oztrak's oldest son had been much the same way.

Erek finished issuing orders to his men and returned to the tent.

"Come," Oztrak said to him. "We'll enjoy tea while I hear your report. Then we'll question your prisoner properly."

They sat on sheepskins while servants brought tea. The Tibetan was dragged to the door of the tent, where he lay huddled on the ground, under guard, whimpering like a lost dog.

"You were gone longer than I expected," Oztrak said to open the conversation. "How did it go?"

"Not well, my commander. I regret to report that Gungor, six of his men, and the interpreter are dead. Even worse, he failed in his mission to bring back Lhalde."

Even in the midst of his shock over the news, Oztrak admired Erek's rigid adherence to military protocol. Most of Oztrak's other officers, far older and more experienced, would have come in babbling the news like fools. Erek had withheld his report until asked, despite the enormity of its content.

Oztrak also noted that Erek labeled the mission as Gungor's failure, not his own.

"How did it happen?" Oztrak asked.

"At first, my commander, we followed your orders to the letter. We patrolled the high plateau until we came to tracks we believed were made by Lhalde's party. They were near Lhalde's designated rendezvous with the Englishman. There we captured two *drokba.* After Gungor put hot irons to them, they confessed that four monks had passed that way two days before. And then, at that point, my commander, Gungor divided his command. He ordered me to take six men and follow Lhalde's back trail in an effort to find the lamasery. I protested, my commander. But Gungor said his six men were more than sufficient to capture four monks. So I obeyed his orders, my commander. Under the circumstances, there was nothing else I could do."

Oztrak was impressed that Erek did not specifically criticize Gungor for dividing his command deep in the land of nonbelievers. Instead, Erek had simply stated facts.

Gungor indeed had acted unwisely. Oztrak himself would never have divided a small patrol so far into the midst of the enemy.

"I followed Lhalde's back trail almost a hundred kilometers westward. There, for ten kilometers and more, the tracks were obliterated by those of hundreds of sheep. For two days I searched, but Lhalde's trail was hidden beneath the tracks of one or another of the herds of sheep. I didn't have the resources to follow all. But I felt that since such precautions had been taken, I undoubtedly was close to the lamasery. So when I came upon one of the herds, I seized the imbecile herdsman and brought him back with me."

"And Gungor?"

"We were to meet at the foot of the mountains, my commander. Where the old caravan route comes on north into Xinjaing. I waited there two days. When Gungor didn't arrive, I made a brief reconnaissance to the east, following his trail. I found where he had destroyed an encampment of *drokba* and taken Lhalde and his monks prisoner. I questioned two of the survivors of that encampment. Through signs and a few phrases, I learned that the day after Gungor was there, two Westerners arrived with guns, hired a tracker, and set out after him. I also followed that old trail. Two days to the west, I found the grave of Gungor and his men. They had all been shot."

Erek handed Oztrak an empty cartridge case. It was of the type used by the Red Chinese in automatic weapons but of a different make.

"The Westerners," Oztrak said. "Americans?"

"I was told that one was American, and the other an Englishman."

Oztrak considered that shard of intelligence.

Could it have been Loomis and Owenby?

Surely the thought was preposterous. Takla Pishan was to have eliminated them in the pass on the border of Nepal before they could set foot in Tibet.

But Oztrak reflected that he had not yet heard from Pishan on the success of his mission. Could Pishan have failed?

"The *drokba* claimed that Lhalde was rescued alive by the two Westerners," Erek went on. "They said the Westerners had come back to that place to retrieve yaks and baggage left there. The new trail made by the Westerners led off slightly south of west. I considered following them. But they had too great a head start. I had with me only six exhausted men on six worn-out horses. Our supplies were gone, and Gungor had destroyed all the food in the *drokba* encampment. With Lhalde's practice of using sheep herds to destroy his tracks, I felt my chances of success were not good. I thought it far more important, my commander, that you know what happened and that I bring in the imbecile so he could be questioned properly."

"You did well, my son," Oztrak said.

If Erek noticed that Oztrak had called him son, he was too adroit to offer the slightest indication.

"I think the imbecile knows something," Erek said. "I can see it in his eyes. It goes beyond his terror."

Oztrak did not relish what he now had to do. Usually he delegated these details to his men. But this interrogation was too important to leave to others.

"Have him brought in," he said.

Erek signaled. Two of his men literally carried the sheepherder into the tent. The man had wet and soiled his trousers, front and back. Apparently his legs no longer would support him. The guards propped him on a low stool, where he sat trembling in fright.

Erek introduced the interpreter, who stood to one side.

Oztrak looked up at the interpreter. "Follow my words closely," he ordered. "Don't soften anything I say. And repeat the words of the Tibetan back to me exactly as he says them, as accurately as possible."

The interpreter acknowledged the order.

Oztrak studied the Tibetan for a long moment in silence. The man's eyes blinked convulsively every few seconds and he wore the perpetual frown of the mentally incompetent, forever attempting to understand the world around them.

"Do you know any monks?" Oztrak asked quietly. "Buddhist monks?"

The imbecile shook his head violently, blinking uncontrollably. "I don't know where the monks live," he mumbled.

Oztrak and Erek exchanged glances.

Oztrak again spoke softly but more forcefully.

"Listen to me. You know how a boa is made into a yak? By cutting off his testicles? That also can be done to a man who won't give the proper answer to questions he is asked. Surely you know that when a sheep is butchered, the intestines spill out on the ground. A man can live a long time—hours, even days—with his intestines at his feet. We don't want to take these measures with you. But we must have correct answers to our questions. Do you understand?"

The imbecile again started whimpering. Tears ran down his face. "I don't know anything about the caves," he said.

Caves? Again Oztrak and Erek exchanged glances.

Never before had Oztrak considered that possibility. Caves were almost nonexistent in those mountains. For more than a year Oztrak had been searching for a stone lamasery, something resembling those that once stood outside Lhasa. Not once had he suspected that the lamasery might be underground, literally.

But the possibility made sense. It would explain why the location of the lamasery had remained such a well-kept secret for such a long time.

"Where are the caves?" Oztrak asked.

"I don't know," the imbecile said through the interpreter.

Oztrak hesitated. Perhaps the threats he had made thus far were ill-considered. The imbecile was showing too much courage. As a sheepherder, he undoubtedly castrated hundreds of animals every year. He would have seen them slaughtered. Even death lacked sufficient terror. But as a shepherd, the imbecile would be required to walk many miles each day.

Walking, not his testicles, was essential in his life.

"Listen to me," Oztrak said again. "See that man

standing there with a rifle? Unless you tell us all we want to know about the caves, he will crush both of your knees with the butt of that gun and you will spend the rest of your life crawling around on the ground like a cockroach."

The Tibetan's whimpers instantly rose in volume, and Oztrak knew he had touched a basic fear. He nodded to the man with the rifle, who stepped forward and drove the butt into the imbecile's right leg, shattering the kneecap. The imbecile screamed and fell to the floor of the tent.

Oztrak gave him a full minute of agony before gesturing for him to be returned to the stool.

"I am merciful," Oztrak told the Tibetan through the interpreter. "Now you are a cripple. You still have one leg. With the help of crutches, you can still walk. But unless you tell us the location of the caves, I'll now turn you into a cockroach."

The Tibetan was in too much pain to speak. He raised a hand, warding off the next blow, surrendering.

"How far are the caves from where we found you?" Oztrak asked. "And in what direction?"

The answer came in disjointed phrases. "A half day. Toward the setting sun. In the mountains."

"What part of the mountains? Describe how you get there."

The information came slowly, in fragments. South end of the mountains. Three ridges. The cave entrance was between the two ridges on the east.

"You lie!" Oztrak said. "There are no mountains there! No caves!"

He gestured. Again the rifle butt was raised. The Tibetan screamed even louder, held up a hand to ward off the blow, and released a torrent of words.

"He says he has helped carry milk and cheese into the caves many times," the interpreter said. "He says the mouth of the cave is difficult to see, because it is well hidden. But he insists that it is there. He swears it."

"Where are the other entrances?"

"He says there is only one."

Oztrak ordered his map case brought to him. He searched until he found the one he wanted. As he spread it on the sheepskin, Erek leaned forward and pointed.

"We found the imbecile about here. These mountains would be about a half day's journey to the west, if one were driving a herd of sheep."

Oztrak studied the map. The detail was not adequate for determining if three ridges extended from the south end, as the Tibetan claimed.

"What do you think?" he asked Erek.

"I tend to believe he's telling the truth. He's not intelligent enough to invent."

Oztrak tended to agree. Yet, he needed more—much more—before he could commit himself and his men to a full-scale operation on the Tibetan high plateau.

Who were the two Westerners who had killed Gungor? Could it possibly have been Loomis and Owenby? And if not, why had Pishan not reported yet with the results of his ambush in the pass?

Oztrak was impatient to move south and destroy the Kamala Lama lamasery. It was the only large concentration of Buddhism remaining in the region. Its destruction would provide an excellent start for the *jihad,* with the goal of destroying all Buddhists in Tibet.

Yet he was faced with an unavoidable delay. He must now go into the Turpan region to raise money. Unlike Iran and other parts of the world, the Islamic faith in Xinjiang was poorly organized and mostly dependent on the populations of small villages.

Oztrak could not understand the apathy of the larger cities for the *jihad.* He himself felt the inexorable pull of the centuries. His ancestors had come into Xinjiang in the thirteenth century, killed all the Buddhists in the region, pulled down the temples, and converted the entire province to Islam.

Now, eight centuries later, the work was still to be finished.

Thus far, no national leader had emerged from under the restraints of the Red Chinese to mobilize the fervor that Oztrak knew was there sleeping. He easily could see himself in such a role, even though politics, crowds, and speeches were against his nature. He vastly preferred open spaces and fighting.

But the fund-raising must be done. He had gathered fifteen hundred young men under his command, all sworn to sacrifice their lives to the *jihad.* He had formed them into military-style squadrons, armed them, and trained them. Now he must have ammunition and supplies for the invasion of Tibet.

Also, he must secure the cooperation of the principal Red Chinese officials in Turpan. Privately he had been told that as long as he was doing their work in clearing the region of Buddhists, the government would not interfere with his *jihad.* Yet he must keep them informed, confide to key officials that he was preparing to take a small army into the high plateau of Tibet.

Moreover, he needed to use the telephone, and the closest one was in Turpan. He despised the instrument and was reluctant to talk on it, but he recognized it as a marvelous invention. It gave him seven league boots. From Turpan he could consult with his sources in Kathmandu and elsewhere, determine what needed to be done, and issue the orders.

It had been through the telephone that he first had learned that Owenby was preparing to smuggle thirty Kalashnikovs and an American into western Tibet. Even while talking on the accursed instrument, Oztrak had made an assessment.

Who else in western Tibet but Lhalde would be buying modern weapons? And who was the American? Surely he must be an expert hired to train Lhalde's warrior monks in the use of those weapons.

Oztrak had planned the ambush in the pass and issued the orders even before he had finished talking over the phone with Takla Pishan.

It would be done, Pishan had said. He promised that he would wait for Owenby in the last pass on the border of Nepal and Tibet, kill the American, and seize the guns.

On that same day Oztrak had made other calls. It had taken him longer, but he had ascertained that the American was named Loomis and that he was indeed a mercenary warrior. Who else in western Tibet could be hiring him but Lhalde? All of the guerrilla fighting against the Red Chinese was concentrated far to the east, in and around Lhasa.

Oztrak had been pleased to have his initial judgment confirmed with the identification of the American. Pishan's ambush in the pass would eliminate the threat of the guns and of the American.

Also while on the telephone to Kathmandu, Oztrak had learned Owenby's exact destination. One of Owenby's yak handlers had told his family, who had not kept the secret. The destination had become common knowledge among traders in Kathmandu, and Oztrak soon learned of it.

He had assumed that Lhalde's rendezvous with Owenby and the American would not be at the lamasery, but at some remote location. He had sent Gungor and Erek into the high plateau to intercept and to interrogate Lhalde's party and, if necessary, to backtrack Lhalde in an effort to locate the hidden lamasery.

But apparently all had not worked out as he had expected. If Owenby and the American were still alive, obviously Pishan's ambush in the pass had failed. Owenby was not enough of a fighter to thwart Pishan. So it must have been the American. Erek had said that Gungor and his men were stalked and killed in their camp on the high plateau. Owenby possessed neither the will nor the ability to take on a man like Gungor in open combat. So it also must have been the American who killed Gungor and his men.

Oztrak prided himself in being a realist. Now he must face facts. Fourteen devout followers of the faith were dead, including two of his best *jihad* commanders—Pishan and Gungor—and the American was still alive.

He reflected that he had made one lamentable mistake: he had underestimated this American, Loomis. Plainly he needed to know more about him. There was no other way: he must go use the telephone, even though he vastly would prefer to be out on the Tibetan high plateau, where there were no telephones and a man was measured by his deeds, not his words.

He was aware of criticism among his commanders that he treated Erek as a son. But Gungor was dead and must be replaced. Oztrak could not imagine the post going to anyone but Erek.

"I must go to Turpan," he told Erek. "Before I go, I'll issue the order for our six arms of the *jihad* to assemble here. From this moment, you will replace Gungor as second-in-command."

Erek did not seem surprised. He genuflected. "I'm most honored, my commander. I'll dedicate my life to proving that you haven't made an error in choosing me."

"All I ask is that you pay more attention to your duties and less to the women. You'll be in charge while I'm gone to Turpan. I want you to train the squadrons, get them ready for the field. When I return, in less than two weeks, we'll go into the Chang Tang, destroy Lhalde, his lama, and his lamasery. Then we will make a sweep through western Tibet killing all Buddhists for the continuing glory of Islam."

"I shall look forward to that with pleasure," Erek said. He gestured. "What about the imbecile?"

Oztrak glanced at the miserable wretch, still whimpering on the floor of the tent. "Put him out of his misery," he said. "Or give him back to your men for sport. Do as you please. We have no further use for him."

7

"As you've no doubt assumed, the caves are not natural," Lhalde said. "From a small indenture in this face of the mountain, a recess no more than a dozen paces square, we hollowed out the rest. The work has continued through thirty years. The dirt was taken out each night and spread on the plain to hide the construction. Grass grew up through it, and it became a part of the plain. I doubt our project could have been evident from the plain or the air at any time."

Loomis, Lhalde, and Owenby stood on a ridge a hundred yards from the main entrance to the lamasery. From that distance the cave opening was almost imperceptible.

The day was clear and sunny, even a trifle warm, unusual for late summer at this altitude. During the week-long trip across the plains, the wounds on Lhalde's face had healed considerably. Loomis did not know the condition of the burns on his chest. Lhalde had not mentioned them, and Loomis had not asked.

Ever since their arrival on the previous evening, Lhalde had been closeted with the Kamala Lama. Now he was taking Loomis and Owenby on a tour of the lamasery and its approaches, so Loomis could make an assessment on the possibilities for defense.

From where they stood, at the south end of the mountain range, three large ridges fanned out like the talons of an eagle. The cave entrance was located between the two on the left.

Earlier in the day Loomis had climbed to the top of the mountain in order to gain a better perspective. The landform around the mountain was perfectly flat. He found that on clear days hundreds of square miles of surrounding country could be monitored from the mountaintop. That was a plus. With lookouts posted, the lamasery would not be taken by surprise.

With a professorial air, Lhalde walked down the slope ahead of Loomis and Owenby, calmly talking as if teaching a class of graduate students.

"For a time fresh air was our greatest concern. Oxygen was in short supply, especially for our lamps. But eventually we succeeded in tunneling through to the other side of the mountain. We installed louvered baffles. Now we control air flow throughout the lamasery."

Loomis thus far had seen only a portion of the underground facilities. He had found the caves dry, warm, and surprisingly comfortable. Most of the monks lived in small cells off the main corridors. Meeting halls, dining rooms, and shrines were scattered about the elaborate subterranean labyrinth.

"We try to keep our contacts with the outside world to a minimum," Lhalde went on. "Usually we manage with only three or four trips a year for whatever supplies absolutely must be purchased. On each trip in and out, the loyal *drokba* drive herds of sheep over our tracks, obliterating all trace. Local supplies—yogurt, cheese, meat—are brought in at night from the *drokba* encampments nearby. Again, sheep are driven over the tracks. For three decades we've succeeded in keeping the location of the lamasery a secret."

Owenby raised an eyebrow. "Yes, but until now no one

has been in much of a dither trying to find it. The Chinese had their hands full with the risings in Lhasa and Rikaze. They weren't about to launch a full-scale search to find out what happened to three hundred monks."

Lhalde acknowledged the point with a nod.

Loomis stopped and looked back at the cave, trying to view the terrain as an invader might see it. "Ever see planes, helicopters?" he asked.

"Very seldom. Rarely we see an airplane in the distance. But never helicopters."

That figured. The mountain range was almost a thousand miles from the military airfields in eastern Tibet. The distance, prevailing headwinds, and altitude ruled out helicopters, except on a high-risk basis. Air search also would be impractical, given the vastness of the terrain. From the air any movement around the mountains would appear to be that of *drokba* tending their herds. Loomis doubted the Red Chinese posed any significant threat to the lamasery. The Communists had neither sufficient forces nor equipment in western Tibet to conduct ground searches of these barren areas.

"Now that you've seen the exterior of the lamasery, what do you think of its defensibility?" Lhalde asked.

Loomis considered the question carefully. Until now, its best defense had been its remoteness, and secrecy. But under the pressures of an active search, secrecy might be the first casualty. Loomis felt he must operate on that assumption.

"Owenby and I can establish a defense perimeter and train your men," Loomis said. "We can try for concealment. But a proper defense will require trenches, barricades, gun emplacements. It'd be a tradeoff against the secrecy you've maintained."

Lhalde frowned. "Would there be any way of setting up a defense some distance away from the lamasery? Perhaps divert an assault *away* from the caves? I'm thinking of the safety of the Kamala Lama."

"We could. But it's not a feasible option," Loomis told him. "We don't have enough men. In order to fight a pitched battle elsewhere, we'd have to strip all defense from the lamasery. The open terrain isn't suitable for committing small forces. When you can see for miles, there's no hope of using the elements of evasion and surprise. Any diversionary force would probably be a sacrifice and, again, we don't have enough men for that."

"Then you'd place guns here? Near the entrance?"

Loomis nodded. "From these ridges, a few well-armed, well-trained men could hold out against four or five times their own number. I don't yet know what's possible in the way of firepower. I must talk with your men, see what can be done with them on minimal training. My biggest concern right now is that we're so limited in equipment. Thirty rifles simply aren't enough. We don't have ammunition for a protracted firefight, let alone much training. For a proper defense, we need mortars, grenades, land mines, machine guns, ammunition."

Lhalde seemed troubled. Loomis gathered the defense of the lamasery was a much bigger project than he had anticipated. "We have explosives, if that would help," he said.

"What kind?"

"Some blasting powder of our own make. In digging the caves, we kept encountering rock. We researched old Chinese manuscripts, found formulas, and manufactured explosives in order to shatter the rocks. Two of our monks have become quite adept."

Loomis reasoned that gunpowder made with a five-hundred-year-old formula would be better than none. Anyone who could manufacture explosives powerful enough to crack boulders no doubt also could make grenades, land mines, and possibly rockets.

"I'll want to talk with your explosives experts," he said.

"Then you believe the lamasery can be defended from here?" Lhalde asked.

"Marginally," Loomis said. "The question is against how many. Do you have any idea what size force we might face?"

Lhalde walked along with his arms folded, his hands tucked into the opposite sleeve. "I've only heard vague rumors, from frightened villagers. They claim that more than a thousand men have been recruited and trained for the *jihad.*"

"Frankly, if it's anywhere near that number, I believe you should consider abandoning the lamasery, at least temporarily," Loomis told Lhalde. "That would be the only safe way. Perhaps the monks could scatter, take refuge among the *drokba.*"

Lhalde hesitated, as if considering what argument to present next. "Come," he said. "I'll show you what is at stake."

He led the way back to the entrance and into the lamasery.

Loomis followed Lhalde and Owenby down a flight of steps. They walked along the wide, stone-lined main corridor. Owenby kept looking up apprehensively.

"No need to worry," Lhalde told him. "The ceilings are quite safe. It's true we had difficulty during our early years here, with two regrettable tragedies. We had no timber or steel to shore up the walls and ceilings, and they kept collapsing. But eventually we looked into some old manuscripts and more or less reinvented the vaulted arch. About thirty of our monks became superb stonemasons. In time they learned to dig and line about two meters of tunnel a day. We haven't had a single collapse in the last twenty-five years—not since we started using the vaulted arch."

Owenby did not appear relieved. "Then maybe you're overdue. I can't imagine what's holding those bloody stones up there."

Lhalde went into a long explanation of how the immense weight pushing down on the interlocking stones worked to make the ceilings even stronger.

Loomis paid little attention to the lecture. He was busy familiarizing himself with the underground layout.

The main corridor was flanked by cells and larger rooms. Here and there monks were assembled, seated in the lotus position, meditating or working their prayer wheels.

The air was musty but oddly pleasant. Tapers burned at spaced intervals of fifteen or twenty feet, giving the corridor and the interior the constant aura of twilight.

Loomis had assumed that Lhalde was headed for the larger meeting halls, deep within the underground complex. But abruptly he turned into a narrow corridor Loomis had not previously noticed. He led the way past a succession of monk cells, then descended another set of steps.

They emerged in a moderately large room, perhaps twenty by thirty feet. A dozen or more monks knelt at small, low desks. Some were poring over old books. Others were writing with nib-tipped pens on old parchment. So great was their concentration that not one looked up. Lhalde walked past them to a solid metal door. He turned and spoke quietly to Loomis and Owenby.

"You gentlemen will be the first outsiders in six centuries to lay eyes on what you are now about to see."

He knocked softly on the door in rhythmic code. From inside came the sound of a heavy bar lifting. Slowly the door creaked open.

A wizened, ancient monk stood staring up at them. In his hand he held a crude cast-iron lantern. The skin of his face was so sunken and wrinkled that Loomis was certain he was at least a hundred years old. The interior of the room was in darkness. Lhalde spoke to the old man for a moment in Tibetan, then made introductions.

"This is Zampo. I suppose his title would translate roughly as our head librarian. He has been in charge of our treasures for more than a half century."

The old man went about the room lighting tapers from

the flame of his lamp. As his eyes adjusted, Loomis saw that the room was filled with rolls of parchment and vellum stacked on tiers of shelves. Hundreds upon hundreds of rolls assumed shape in the dim light.

"Normally this room is kept in darkness to protect the manuscripts," Lhalde said. "Zampo knows precisely where to go with his small lantern to find what he wants. So this lighting is rare, and an occasion."

The gnarled little gnome of a man came to stand respectfully before Lhalde, who again spoke to him briefly in Tibetan. Zampo turned, went to a far shelf, and took down a roll of vellum. He brought it to Lhalde and handed it to him with great care.

"This is an epistle of the Apostle Paul to the Romans—a manuscript unknown to the Christian canon," Lhalde said. He unrolled a foot or more of the old vellum. "From several references, it is evident that the letter was written from the Iberian Peninsula. As you both no doubt know, there is a Christian tradition that Saint Paul went on an evangelical mission to Spain in his final years, before he returned to Rome and was martyred. But proof has been lacking. This manuscript offers sound evidence of his evangelical mission to Spain. It also is invaluable for its presentation of Paul's thinking on the fledgling church during the final portion of his life. I'm confident most Pauline scholars would quickly recognize the letter's authenticity."

Zampo handed him another roll.

"This manuscript is the earliest version extant of the Book of Luke. As you know, Saint Luke was the only writer of the Gospel to describe the birth, boyhood, and early life of Jesus. But from Christ's twelfth year, when he confounded the elders in the temple, accounts of the remainder of his late childhood and early manhood have been lost. We next hear of Jesus when he is a man past thirty, setting out on his evangelical preaching." Lhalde unrolled a portion of the text and smiled. "Here Saint Luke tells us that Jesus went into what is now India and became associated with the great religious leaders and thinkers there. This revelation is priceless. It explains why Christ's fundamental Jewish faith was imbued with an overlay of Eastern mysticism and why he was so persecuted by his fellow Jews. This manuscript contains an extensive account of the lost years. This portion obviously was removed from the Gospels by councils of the early church. I can't overstate the effect this manuscript would have on Christian scholarship throughout the world. It opens up possibilities of what was in the so-called Q document, the missing account from which all the Gospels were in part derived. We have part of the Q document here, but not all."

He laughed, interrupting himself. "Forgive me. You can see that all of this is close to my heart. These manuscripts are priceless not only to Buddhism but to all of the world's religions. We have an early version of the *Bhagavad-Gita,* containing portions long lost to Vedic scholars. We have other writings by Vyasa, the assumed author of the *Gita.* Name a major religion, and we have similar treasures. In our quest for knowledge, we have assembled early materials from every faith. I have mentioned the specifics bearing on Christianity because as Christians you well can appreciate the value of these treasures."

"I can't speak for Loomis," Owenby said. "But as for me, perhaps you should say 'Christians of a sort.'" He glanced at Loomis, including him in the joke.

Loomis did not respond. All of Lhalde's revelations held deep meaning for him. He had been reared in a strict Protestant home where Bible instruction came with the ABC's.

"Interestingly enough, the manuscripts of both Luke and John contain a number of Christ's references to reincarnation," Lhalde went on. "References even more specific than those few that slipped past the early church censors and made their way into the New Testament. Plainly Jesus accepted reincarnation, as did the early Christian church. Certainly Origen, the greatest Christian theologian of the early church, regarded reincarnation as fact. I wish we had more time to explore this line of thought, for it would be most appropriate to the occasion."

"How so?" Loomis asked.

Lhalde carefully rerolled the priceless manuscript of the Book of Luke and returned it to Zampo.

"Because, Mr. Loomis, late this evening you are to meet with the Kamala Lama." He turned and studied Loomis with undisguised curiosity. "You will be the first outsider he has spoken with in thirty years. He made the request himself to see you. This is most strange, for when he asked me to bring you to him, neither I, nor anyone else, had yet informed him that you were here."

8

Loomis was deeply moved by the old manuscripts. He was familiar enough with church history to recognize the worth of the Christian documents alone. He had no doubt that what he had been shown would have a tremendous dramatic impact on Christendom—probably the greatest since the Dead Sea Scrolls came to light more than a half century ago.

He remembered Lhalde's quiet determination, in their first meeting, when he pounded a sheepskin with a long, bony finger and declared that the documents "must not be destroyed."

Now Loomis found himself consumed by the same fervor. He felt that despite the odds, he must find some way to save the monastery, and its priceless treasures.

He asked to see the rest of the underground facilities. Lhalde took Loomis and Owenby on a complete tour.

Loomis soon learned that the lamasery functioned like a fine-tuned machine. With no more than the occasional soft whisper of a gong, the monks went to their assigned tasks. Traffic and confusion was kept to a minimum. Most of the monks maintained an imposed silence throughout the day, and Loomis was impressed by the aura of tranquillity that lay over the entire monastery.

Lhalde first led them through the factory areas, where monks were at work with looms and spinning wheels.

"We make all of our own cloth," Lhalde said. "With wool so abundant, the process is rather simple. Virtually all of our sewing is done by hand, as we have done it for centuries."

In an adjoining room weavers were producing rugs and blankets. In a leather shop, craftsmen were producing boots, shoes, and sandals.

"We've been tempted to sell some of our excess goods outside, but unfortunately the risk is too great," Lhalde said. "So we have stored our surplus away, against future use."

Six artists were creating *thang-kas,* the art form depicting facets of Buddhism and Hinduism.

"The word *thang-ka* means 'written record,'" Lhalde explained to Loomis. "We like to consider them a representation of faith in visual terms. The mandala—circle—suggests the universe, the wheel of life. Most of the paintings in the surrounding square portray significant periods of the Buddha's life. Here he is a Hindu prince, innocent, protected from the harshness of the world by his father. Here he sees the sufferings of others. Here he wanders seven years in the forest, seeking truth, while tempted by the evil one, Mara. Then we see him here meditating under the bodhi tree, where he received his inspiration and rose as the Buddha, or enlightened one."

Loomis had seen the *thang-kas* in every monk's cell, and an abundance in the dining halls and prayer rooms. Along with a generous use of rugs, the *thang-kas* helped to soften the bare stone walls throughout the monastery.

"We have sold *thang-kas* to the tourist market in Kathmandu and Lhasa from time to time," Lhalde said. "They are easily transported, and the risk of their being traced seems minimal."

Lhalde then took Loomis and Owenby down to the

storerooms where grain, manufactured goods, and supplies were kept in darkness.

"Down here the temperature and humidity remain constant," Lhalde said. "We have virtually no spoilage."

He took them through the kitchens where food was prepared for all three hundred fifty monks, and to the dining halls, where the monks ate in shifts.

Loomis asked how the cooking fires were kept hidden.

"The stoves are vented through a shaft to the west face of the mountain," Lhalde explained. "In cooking, we use only animal fats for fuel, for they burn with less visible smoke. The fumes are diffused by the wind."

They passed room after room where monks sat meditating or turning their prayer wheels.

"Every monk spends many hours fulfilling the requirements of a religious life," Lhalde said. "In addition, he has other duties—work in the factory rooms, cleaning the corridors, tending the lamps, preparing food. Everyone has menial chores to perform."

They came to a room where six warrior monks were training. Stripped to the waist, they were practicing body throws. Loomis recognized a wide mixture of martial arts.

Lhalde introduced the instructor, Khedru, head of the warrior monks. He appeared to be in his late thirties, and was taller and larger than most Tibetans. He had a slow, easy smile and a direct gaze that Loomis liked. On Lhalde's suggestion, Khedru led his warriors through a demonstration of their martial skills. Loomis noted that all holds, throws, and blows were defensive, not lethal.

He was pleased to see that the warrior monks were well muscled and in superb physical shape. He asked about their bronzed skin. Most of the monks in the lamasery were pale as the result of their life underground.

"We recognize that subterranean dwelling isn't healthy physically or psychologically and that sunshine and fresh air are necessary," Lhalde answered. "So each monk spends several days each month outside, working with the *drokba.* Since health is especially essential to the warrior monks, they are authorized to spend even more time outside. Most take advantage of the privilege."

"What weapons are they trained to use?" Loomis asked.

Lhalde hesitated. "Clubs. Staves. Fists."

"But not guns?"

Lhalde did not appear eager to answer. "Perhaps we haven't been completely realistic in this regard. The warriors have had no training whatsoever in guns."

"Dear God," Owenby said. He shook his head in bewilderment. For once words seemed to fail him.

Loomis also was jolted. But he had thirty Kalashikovs, and he would need someone to put them to good use. The warrior monks were the only candidates.

"Tell Khedru we must start work with his warriors immediately, training them to use the guns. Tell him to break his group into ten-man squads. We can begin this afternoon."

Lhalde translated, and Khedru replied that he would have his men ready. He and Loomis shook hands and agreed to meet at one o'clock.

Lhalde led Loomis and Owenby back into the main corridor. "I believe you've now seen everything," he said. "All except the Kamala Lama's private quarters, just off the library. You'll be his guest there this evening."

"What about the ventilation shaft?" Loomis asked.

"It's at the end of the main corridor. There's still some construction work going on, and there's not much to see. But we can take a look, if you wish."

"I do," Loomis said.

They walked to the end of the corridor. There it narrowed. For the next hundred yards, the shaft was hardly more than three feet wide and less than six high. With bodies bent and heads lowered, they walked down the length of the dark tunnel, with a steady breeze blowing against their faces. Ahead, Loomis could see daylight.

An arrangement of wooden louvers blocked the end of the passageway. Loomis helped Lhalde set them partially aside. With the resistance of the baffles reduced, the volume of air moving through the tunnel increased.

"From here we can control the flow of air throughout the lamasery," Lhalde said. "Otherwise, on windy days it would be quite fierce, enough to extinguish the lamps and blow papers about."

From the passageway they emerged into a spherically shaped, rock-lined terminus. Sunlight streamed through an iron grate Loomis assumed was used to keep out wild animals.

"What's on the other side of the grate?" he asked.

"Nothing," Lhalde said. "The opening is at the foot of a cliff on the mountain. A ridge projects out from it. The opening can't be seen from below. It could be found only by stumbling on it accidentally."

"Has this opening ever been used as an entrance?"

"Never. We decided early that for security reasons the airshaft should not be used for foot traffic. Movement this high on the side of the mountain might attract attention. Also, we need to protect the integrity of the baffles, in order to keep the air flow constant."

"This took a lot of engineering," Loomis said. "Do you have maps, drawings of the mountain range, the tunnel layout?"

Lhalde frowned. "I believe so. That was several years ago. Zampo would know where to find them."

They walked back through to the library. Within minutes Zampo located a sheaf of yellowed drawings.

Loomis searched through them until he found a detailed map of the mountain range. He moved to a corner so he would not disturb the other monks. There he lay the map on one of the low desks.

"Where are the *drokba* encamped?" he asked.

Lhalde studied the map for a moment, then pointed. "The largest is here."

It was on the same side of the mountain as the entrance to the lamasery and about halfway toward the far end of the range. Loomis estimated the distance as three miles.

"And the others?"

Lhalde leaned over the map. "Here, and here."

Both were on the other side of the mountain—one at the far end and the other not far from the air-shaft opening.

Loomis marveled at the ingenuity of the arrangement. From those bases the nomads grazed their flocks over hundreds of square miles of grassland. Even the closest observer would never suspect that they served as a larder for a hidden monastery containing three hundred fifty monks.

Loomis took the map with him to study, along with several drawings of the internal layout of the monastery.

He did not quite know yet how it all fitted together. But he knew that from these basic elements he somehow must build a defense adequate to repel a thousand invaders.

Owenby had been building toward an outburst for more than an hour. Loomis was coming to know him well enough to recognize the signs. He kept quiet and waited. At last Owenby came out with it.

"All things considered, Loomis, I think we'd bloody well cut out of this deal while we can. It's daft! There's not even a single bugger here who has ever fired a rifle. It's a losing proposition from the word go."

They were at the tip of the ridge to the left of the lamasery entrance. Loomis was drawing a contour map of the terrain, choosing the best positions for his outposts.

"You're free to leave any time," Loomis told him. "Nobody's holding you."

"Leave by myself?" Owenby shook his head. "Don't you know there are bandits out there? Alone, I'd never make it to the border of Nepal, let alone to Kathmandu." He remained silent for a moment, watching Loomis make notes on his map. "But I'm not the dumbest fellow in the world. I've been putting a lot together during the last few days."

"Like what?" Loomis asked.

"Like what Pishan was doing in that pass. Plainly he was waiting for us, and no one else. You do follow me, don't you? That old trail is hardly used anymore. Two caravans a week could be considered a traffic jam. With the wind and altitude, no one dallies in that pass, especially in a snowstorm, and especially toward night. I now doubt that Pishan's being there was a chance encounter, like I first thought. I think he went into that pass ahead of us and waited."

"I figured that a week ago," Loomis told him.

The revelation seemed to irritate Owenby. "Well, hell, I knew the sod, trusted him. You've got to give me that. I still find it bloody difficult to believe he'd murder a friend, unless there was something else involved. Not for thirty rifles he wouldn't want."

"Why not?"

"Well, mind you, the Uighurs prefer those old Mauser-type bolt actions. They distrust automatics and semiautomatics. It's a bloody mind-set, like the way your American coppers prefer revolvers when most of the world's policemen carry semiautomatic pistols. The Uighurs believe, rightly or wrongly, that automatic weapons won't function well in the sandstorms and arid conditions in the Xinjiang Province. They say the bolt actions are easier to keep clean and can be cleared quicker when they jam."

"They could be right." Loomis had completed his sketch of the ridge. He started another of the opposite ridge and the plain below. A vague suspicion crossed his mind. "How well did you know Pishan?"

"Moderately well, actually. I took perhaps a dozen orders from him. Nothing big, but nothing small, either. He'd call and want two or three hundred rifles delivered to western Nepal, somewhere along the border of Tibet. Later I made four trips to Turpan with goods for him."

"He say who the guns were for?"

"Not precisely. The bugger hinted at resistance groups in Afghanistan, Pakistan, the Xinjiang Province itself. I believed him. He gave me no cause not to. Oh, I heard wild rumors. But they're common in my trade. I paid no attention to them."

Loomis could see that Owenby had something to confess, but did not want to do so voluntarily.

"What rumors?" Loomis asked.

Owenby frowned. "Well, once I was told Pishan was mixed up in the *jihad.* At the time, don't you see, it didn't make sense. He didn't seem the type. But now I'm wondering. Suppose Pishan was ordered to take us out in the pass. Then it follows that the people who kidnapped Lhalde wouldn't be expecting us, so they didn't sit around and wait for us to walk into a trap. That's why we were able to surprise them later. They thought we'd already been eliminated."

Loomis nodded. "That's the way I have it figured."

Owenby appeared even more unhappy with this further evidence that Loomis was ahead of him in thinking. "Well, shit. I suppose you're considering me incredibly gullible and naive. Maybe I have been. But I don't make a bloody habit of it. And right now I'm remembering those rumors in Xinjiang Province—rumors I mostly ignored at the time. After all that's happened, I think we'd best pay some attention to them."

Loomis finished and folded his second hand-drawn map. He looked at Owenby and waited.

"They say in Turpan that a man by the name of Oztrak has placed a tax on all the little villages in the Turpan Sink in order to finance a holy war. I find it difficult to believe the sod could raise much money. All those villages are indescribably poor. But there you are. They say he commands fifteen hundred men, well mounted and well trained. I scoffed at the number. I thought it a ridiculous exaggeration, but maybe not. I've sold six hundred or more rifles in that region myself, along with a ton of ammunition. Maybe it all went to Oztrak. Hell, I don't know."

Again he was silent for a time. Again Loomis waited.

"I've been going over it all in my head," Owenby went on. "Pishan buying all those weapons. Trying to kill us in the pass. The kidnapping of Lhalde and the murders of his monks. Oztrak and his holy war. I see a strong possibility they're all connected."

"I'm sure they are," Loomis said.

Owenby seemed not to have heard. "So now I'm coming to grips with what no doubt are the realities, old sod." He pointed. "Can you imagine fifteen hundred mounted men out there on that plain charging your thirty monks who never before have fired a rifle?"

Loomis did not bother to answer the question. "Mounted how?" he asked.

"On those sturdy little Siberian horses. Fifteen hundred of them. Picture the hordes of Genghis Khan five centuries ago and you'd come close to Oztrak's army."

"How come you've never mentioned the fifteen hundred men before?"

"Like I said, I was so bloody sure it was wild exaggeration. But, mind you, what if it *is* true? And here's something else to consider: every one of those fifteen hundred is eager to die in battle for Islam. They think they win brownie points with Allah for doing so. They're like those Japanese kamikaze pilots in World War Two. Every charge they'd make would be a suicide charge."

Loomis stood looking at the plain below. If Owenby's figures were anywhere near accurate, the situation indeed appeared hopeless.

"So I think we should get out of this deal now, while we can," Owenby said again. "I keep remembering that old nursery school rhyme, 'Run away, run away, fight again another day.' I only lost my shirt in the bean episode. In this I have the uncomfortable feeling I'm about to lose my ass."

Loomis did not answer for a time. He stood studying the ridges, the approach to the lamasery entrance, seeking a way to make them impregnable. He thought of the manuscripts and the peaceful tranquillity of the monks as contrasted with the ruthlessness he had seen among their enemies. Surely there must exist some means of saving the monastery and its treasures.

"You've seen those manuscripts," he said to Owenby. "You've heard Lhalde. We can't walk away from this."

Owenby slowly let out a lung full of air in a massive sigh. "You're good at what you do, Loomis. I'll give you that. I could hardly believe it when you took out Pishan and his sods in the pass. One against six! Then I saw you calmly chop down those buggers when we rescued Lhalde. You're very, very good. But Christ on a crutch! That's a bloody *army* coming to destroy this monastery. You've got nothing to work with but a bunch of pacifists who normally wouldn't kill an insect. And you can include me in that category. True, I've now killed two men. But I closed my eyes when I did it. I'm a weak reed in this game. Let's face facts. We don't have a bloody chance!"

Loomis put the maps in his shirt pocket and glanced at his watch. "We'll find a way to even the odds a little. It's one o'clock. Come on. Let's go start training our troops."

9

"You have a most unusual profession, Mr. Loomis," the Kamala Lama said. "I'd like to ask you some questions, if they're not too personal."

The request put Loomis on guard. He spoke cautiously. "I'll do my best."

Loomis and the lama were seated on red and gold silk cushions, facing each other at the end of a long, narrow room. Gold-threaded tapestries and exquisite *thang-kas* shrouded what no doubt were bare rock walls. Ornate cashmere rugs covered the floor. Lhalde had brought Loomis down to the lama's private quarters, introduced him, and then withdrawn, leaving them alone. To Loomis's surprise, the lama spoke excellent English, which he said had been gleaned from long study, Lhalde's tutoring, and habitual monitoring of BBC broadcasts.

From the first, Loomis had been struck by the strange contradictions in the man. He was younger than Loomis had expected, probably no more than forty, and his unblemished face was round and childlike, conveying remarkable innocence and sincerity. Yet his eyes were sharp with intelligence and understanding. His personal magnetism was overwhelming. Loomis did not find it difficult to believe that he truly was in the presence of a saintly person, perhaps even a godly person, as the Buddhist monks believed.

"Do you feel a strong *necessity* to do the work you do, Mr. Loomis?" the Kamala Lama asked. "Are you driven to it, despite an uneasy reluctance?"

The question was indeed too personal. Loomis answered carefully. "I suppose so. Certainly I keep going back to it."

The Kamala Lama held up an unblemished hand and smiled. "Please, Mr. Loomis. I have a reason for asking. Do you find a sense of fulfillment in fighting the battles of others?"

Again Loomis was disinclined to answer. "Sometimes," he said.

"And this is most important. Do you often have the impression that you've done it all before? When you're in battle, do you sense that you're coming home from a far journey?"

Loomis felt a prickling along his spine. The man was uncannily accurate.

"Quite often," he admitted.

From the questions and the insight Loomis now understood that the Kamala Lama was the author of the letter that had brought him here and not Lhalde. This discovery demanded a complete reassessment of the man before him and the entire situation.

"I've always been intrigued with the American wartime general, George Patton," the Kamala Lama went on. "General Patton was convinced that through many lifetimes he had fought in many battles throughout history. His conviction on the subject of reincarnation was most rare for a Western mind. Are you familiar with that facet of him?"

"I am," Loomis said.

Again the lama smiled, for the moment appearing

quite boyish. "Since you've so gracefully humored me on this subject, I'll venture further. I suppose you know it's a common theory that certain sets of entities continue their relationships through many incarnations, many lives. I am among those who believe that this is so. And in this context, Mr. Loomis, I'm convinced that it was no accident that brought you to help us. Lhalde thinks he searched you out. But I'm confident that you were there to find and that your coming here to help us was fated."

Not knowing what to say to that, Loomis remained silent. After a moment, the Kamala Lama continued.

"I'm approaching what I want to say to you by this circuitous route because I know how difficult it would be for most Westerners to believe that I can sit here alone, cut off from mankind, and receive strong impressions of events in other parts of the world. But I sense you are receptive, that you've had experience in this area and possess an open mind."

Loomis indeed had seen strange phenomena in his travels, especially in Haiti, Africa, and the Orient. He nodded his acceptance of the statement.

The lama's sharp eyes were fixed on him. "Lately, Mr. Loomis, I've been deeply troubled by the growing forces arrayed against us—arrayed against Buddhism, against this lamasery. I haven't revealed the depth of my concern to Lhalde or the other monks because I would only alarm them for no purpose. But I now tell you that the entities that would destroy this lamasery have amassed great strength. They are preparing to use it. I know for certain they will be victorious in entering this lamasery."

A long silence fell.

Loomis thought of all his planning and his unsuccessful search for some means to an impregnable defense.

"Is there nothing we can do to stop them?" he asked.

The lama hesitated. "I'm not certain of the final outcome. I only have this vivid impression of the entities sweeping through these corridors." He closed his eyes for a moment, as if seeing this vision. When he spoke again, his eyes remained closed. "And I sense that they are old, old enemies, Mr. Loomis. Eternal enemies. Yours and mine. I'm certain that this is merely another in a long string of battles. Mr. Loomis, you have met this foe many times in the past."

Again Loomis felt prickling along his spine. The flickering tapers, the exotic setting of the small room multiplied the effect of the eerie conversation.

The lama opened his eyes. "I asked to speak with you because I wanted to inform you of these old enemies. Also, I have a request to make of you." He paused. "I'm sure Lhalde and the others will insist that my safety is of primary concern. Please pay no attention to them in this regard. They also will attempt to spare Zampo and other aged and favorite monks among their ranks. I here and now countermand all such requests. Of fundamental importance is the library. It *must* be saved, whatever else is sacrificed. Lives come and go, but knowledge is fragile. Truths can be lost for thousands of years and the loss causes untold suffering. We must preserve the manuscripts at all costs. Do you understand?"

Loomis nodded. The Kamala Lama paused for a long moment.

"Of next concern is the lamasery. Not the physical plant, but the lives and working routine of the monks. My own safety ranks a far distant third. Do I have your concurrence and collusion in this?"

The rankings made sense. Loomis now *knew* that this was the man who called the shots and not Lhalde. He nodded his silent agreement.

"Good." The lama leaned toward Loomis and spoke with special emphasis. "I want you to make all the necessary decisions. I sense that this is *your* battle even more than ours. As you Americans say, you are the key player. Lhalde, the monks, and I are pawns in a contest that was set in motion long ago."

The Kamala Lama was saying what Loomis had sensed from the first, and defined the inexplicable lure that had drawn him into this job. He *had* felt that this coming battle was his even more than that of those in the monastery.

"Most Westerners find reincarnation difficult to accept because they are trained from childhood to think of time as linear," the Kamala Lama continued. "Implicit in the Buddha's enlightenment was his recognition that time is cyclical. The Western concept is that a man is born, lives, dies, in a progression of events, and that if a spiritual state exists, it must lie at the end of that progression. We Buddhists understand that the life of the soul is cyclical, just as are other forms in nature. Time is not a constant. The difference between a second and a thousand years lies only in our perception. In God's view, perhaps they are the same. It is man's conceit that he chooses to measure time."

Again the lama closed his eyes as if meditating. Loomis waited. After a long interval the lama opened his eyes and regarded Loomis with a most serious expression.

"Forgive me, but I sense in you a terrible inner struggle. You are pulled toward the peace and contentment of a consuming love for a person. And yet you are drawn in the opposite direction by these old, uncompleted battles. Please accept my profound gratitude that you have yielded, in this instance, to the call of the past and have come here to assume our burdens."

Loomis was left speechless. He could not have defined better his inner conflicts between his life with Maria Elena and his work.

"I would prefer to talk longer with you, for I find you a most receptive person. But the hour is late. I know you have many things to do. May I?"

He extended a hand. Assuming they were to shake hands, Loomis put out his own. But the lama drew him forward and placed both hands on Loomis's head.

In that instant Loomis was startled by a sudden, diffused sense of warmth spreading through his body. A profound calmness came over him. The feeling deepened. Never before had he been so at peace with himself, yet infused with energy.

The moment—or perhaps minutes—passed. Loomis looked up. The lama's hands again were folded in his lap. His eyes were closed and he seemed to be in a profound trance.

Still under the spell of the strange, mystic experience, Loomis quietly left the room.

Lhalde was waiting outside, at the door of the library. He stood tall and erect, arms folded, hands tucked into the opposite sleeves of his robe.

He gave Loomis an analytical glance in the light of the hall tapers.

"You look different, my friend. I'm not at all surprised. I've never seen anyone not affected by meeting our lama."

Loomis was not yet prepared to talk about it.

Lhalde fell into step and they started back toward the cell where Loomis and Owenby were quartered. On each side of the corridor monks were awake, reciting their mantras, working their prayer wheels.

"We believe that after his many reincarnations, the Kamala Lama is now approaching nirvana," Lhalde said. "Such a godly state is rarely achieved in this world. Did he bless you?"

"I suppose," Loomis said, wanting to know more. "He put his hands on my head."

"Both hands?"

Loomis nodded.

Lhalde gave him a sidelong glance. "Most extraordinary. You should be most honored. Even a one-hand blessing is reserved for other holy men. Outsiders usually are touched only by a tassel."

At an intersection of corridors Lhalde gestured for Loomis to stop. He glanced around them as if to ascertain that they were alone. He lowered his voice.

"I may have bad news. I'm not sure. Perhaps you can judge. In one of the *drokba* camps not far from here there was a young shepherd who was kicked in the head by a horse when he was a boy. He was harmless enough and did his work. But he never regained full use of his mental faculties."

Lhalde paused. The flickering lights gave his face dramatic intensity.

"Ten days ago this young shepherd disappeared while tending his flock. At first it was assumed he might have been killed by a snow leopard. A search was made. No sign was found. Trackers were called in. The site was discovered where the youth was seized by six men on horses. The tracks led off to the north."

Again Lhalde glanced up and down the corridor and lowered his voice even more.

"My friend, this young shepherd knows the location of this lamasery. Under ordinary circumstances, he could be trusted. But if he is frightened out of his wits, and tortured, he may not have the mental capacity to keep the secret. I now fear our location may be known to our enemies."

For the last two days Loomis had been weighing the benefits of trenches and gun emplacements against the risk of concealment. Now, in the wake of Lhalde's news, he no longer could entertain a choice. He would have to go with trenches and barricades.

And if the brain-damaged youth was taken ten days ago, even now the Uighurs might be riding south to do battle. Clearly he had little time to prepare.

"Tomorrow I want the warrior monks free for full-time training," he told Lhalde. "I want to meet with your explosives experts. I want everyone made available who has worked with explosives in the past."

"They'll be freed from all other duties," Lhalde assured him.

"I also want every man freed that you can spare," Loomis insisted. "All three hundred and fifty, if possible. There's much physical labor to be done outside the entrance."

Lhalde frowned. "The work of the lamasery must go

on. I can delegate some of the younger monks to assist you. Perhaps a hundred."

"I need every man," Loomis said again. "Everyone not actually engaged in cooking or other essential duties."

Lhalde hesitated. "I'll see what I can do."

They parted at the entrance to the cell were Loomis and Owenby slept. Loomis entered, took off his boots, and lay down fully clothed. Owenby was already asleep, lying on his back, snoring.

Loomis thought back over his conversation with the Kamala Lama. The man's insights had cut close to the bone. Loomis long had been troubled by the conflicts between his work and his marriage. He had spent many hours worrying over this problem. But never before had he considered that the difficulty might stem from forces outside life itself. He would never have dreamed that his profession might be a carryover from past lives. But it indeed seemed to be a calling he could not escape.

Certainly, this basic schism in his life had always seemed beyond solution. He would have preferred to stay home with Maria Elena. But this obsession for action kept taking him to remote places in the world, to fight for other people's causes. As the Kamala Lama so aptly had described it, when the battles started, he always had this strong feeling that he was coming home, that all else was secondary.

He thought of Lhalde's story about the half-wit shepherd boy. Few men would be able to endure the tortures suffered by Lhalde's assistants. He doubted that the shepherd boy could hold out long without breaking. No doubt by now the secret was out and the location of the lamasery was known.

Loomis lay back and forced himself toward sleep. With daylight he would begin a drastic revision of his defensive strategy.

10

Oztrak welcomed Chang Song and Ramcek into his home. The meeting had been arranged with great delicacy, and Oztrak was determined to be the perfect host despite his feelings. Ushering his guests into the largest and most comfortable room, he supervised his servants carefully as they served a superb blend of tea, accompanied by a sumptuous array of rice cakes.

"You have a lovely home," Chang observed in passable Uighur. "Truly you are a most successful man."

Oztrak stepped carefully around the praise. Riches were never secure in a Communist regime.

"Thank you, Mr. Commissar. Fortunately I learned early to acquire objects I admired, wherever my duties took me. The statuary and vases are from Nepal. The rugs from Afghanistan. The furniture from India. Through the years my work has taken me far afield, Mr. Commissar."

Chang acknowledged that fact with a slight bow of his head. "You have proved most valuable to my government. I hope our relationship will enjoy long life."

It was a generous statement. Oztrak was emboldened.

Although Chang was the number two Red Chinese administrator in Xinjiang Province—in many ways the most powerful, for his duties were totally administrative and he was free of the ceremonial obligations that hampered the chairman.

His post was also less political. Chairmen came and went, but Chang was a survivor. He now had been the Red Chinese resident in Xinjiang twenty-one years, building multifaceted organization of intrigue and authority. One did not take his words lightly.

He was solidly built and of Han extraction. Oztrak estimated that he was in his early fifties. His round face was sallow from too much indoor living, and there was something effete about him despite his preference for Mao-styled military tunics. Oztrak did not like him, but that fact did not preclude doing business with him.

Oztrak had far less respect for Ramcek. Of Uighur descent, Ramcek had long served as a lackey to the Communists, often at the expense of others of his race. He had been Chang's assistant for the last decade.

"We have explored extensively the information you gave us," Chang said, opening the discussion. "During the last few days Delegate Ramcek has made use of our sources in Washington, London, Tokyo, Hong Kong, elsewhere. We have gone to much effort and expense to obtain the information you wish."

"I am most grateful," Oztrak said.

He had not known that Ramcek had been named a delegate to the People's Congress of the so-called autonomous republic. But the appointment was to be expected. It was yet another facet of Chang's far-reaching power, of his ability to assume and to maintain control of every branch of government.

Chang glanced at Ramcek, a clear signal for him to take the floor and present his information.

Ramcek reached into an inner coat pocket and pulled out a notebook. He flipped it open and held it on his knee.

As Ramcek started speaking, Oztrak noted once again

how, after dealing with the Chinese government for years, Ramcek's native Uighur bore an unpleasant Chinese accent. Oztrak was aware that Ramcek made his living by compiling dossiers on individuals for the Chinese government—often derogatory information on his fellow Uighurs.

"I'll capsule the subject's life in chronological order," Ramcek said. "I have assembled a complete report, which I will leave with you. I now will give you only the essential facts."

Oztrak waited while Ramcek got himself organized. Behind Ramcek and Chang, in the garden outside, Oztrak's six living children had come out to play. Their tutor hovered near them in close but unobtrusive attendance. Oztrak watched through the large sliding glass doors as his two oldest living sons squared off with wooden swords, thrusting and hacking at each other in earnest contest. Oztrak studied their skills in the techniques he had taught them.

"Loomis was born and reared in Texas," Ramcek began. "Completed college before the Vietnam War. He went into Vietnam in the early part of the war, as an officer in the Green Berets. Later he served as an intelligence officer with the CIA."

Oztrak grunted in surprise. What was a man of that background doing in Tibet, attempting to defend a small monastery?

"His specialty at that time was in work with mountain guerrilla units," Ramcek went on. "Somewhere in there, about the time of the Diem assassinations, he fell from grace. He opposed CIA policy, tried to block an operation. Two attempts were made by the CIA to eliminate him. He killed the two men assigned to assassinate him. Then he disappeared for a while."

Oztrak was intrigued. Clearly the man himself was a rebel. And Loomis's experiences somewhat paralleled his own. He had served as adviser with mountain fighters in Afghanistan, where his son was killed. He frowned, thinking back. Vietnam. That was a long time ago.

Loomis was not young. He had acquired considerable experience.

Ramcek turned a page of his notebook. "He surfaced next in Africa, as a mercenary working among some insurgents seeking independence. He moved on to Latin America, various countries. Then, in the Dominican Republic, he was serving as chief of security to a dictator when a terrorist group called Hamlet attempted to detonate an atomic bomb. Loomis was instrumental in averting a disaster. Through that incident he apparently was restored to the good graces of the CIA. He won restoration of his American citizenship."

Oztrak found it difficult to keep from showing his astonishment. He remembered the Hamlet incident. A terrorist group had succeeded in assembling and detonating an atomic weapon. It had dominated the news for weeks, even penetrating the backcountry of Afghanistan, where Oztrak had been training Muslim guerrillas.

Ramcek consulted his notes. "It was during the Hamlet incident that Loomis met his future wife, Maria Elena de la Torre. At the time she was a film actress well known in Europe. Since their marriage, she has become an American movie star. They maintain a home in Beverly Hills, California."

Ramcek turned a page. "For a time he was associated with a large aircraft corporation as head of security. In more recent years, he has worked with a Philippine insurrectionist group. Six weeks ago, he flew into Kathmandu, contacted Owenby, and set about acclimating himself to the altitude. You know the rest."

Oztrak sat watching his sons at their sword play, analyzing what he had heard.

An important part was missing from Ramcek's report. Oztrak spoke his thought aloud.

"Why? After such a long career working with governments, political insurgents, and corporations, why would he now hire himself out to a small band of Buddhist monks in the wastelands of the Tibetan plateau? It doesn't make sense."

Ramcek shrugged and shuffled his papers. "The money, I suppose. After all, he's a mercenary. Therein lies the motivation."

Oztrak could not accept that. He spoke more to Chang than to Ramcek. "If he were after money, almost any international conglomerate would pay him more in a year than that Buddhist lamasery is worth." He turned back to Ramcek. "No, there's something else here. Something that you're missing."

Raising his eyebrows, Ramcek did his best to appear offended. He reached into his briefcase for a large packet. "There's much more here in the complete report. I'm sure you'll find what you want."

"What is his religion?" Oztrak asked.

Ramcek hesitated, trying to remember. "Christian. I believe he was reared Protestant. I forget the exact denomination, but it's in there. His wife is Roman Catholic."

Oztrak had never been able to understand how other people could mix religions in their household or extend their friendships to those of other religions. With him religion was his life. Every other consideration was secondary. Yet he sensed that religion had nothing to do with Loomis traveling to Tibet to work with the lamasery.

"What is his relationship now with the CIA?"

"Estranged, I'm told by confidential sources in Washington. But there exists a certain mutual respect. The agency attempted to work with him during the Hamlet incident in the Dominican Republic, and more recently during the insurgency in the Philippines."

"Is there any chance he's working for the CIA? Sent into Tibet on some fact-finding mission?"

"No," Ramcek said emphatically. "I have it on best authority that he no longer performs any services whatsoever for the CIA."

"What are his relations with his wife? Any sign they're at odds?"

"Apparently not. From sources in Nepal, I ascertained

that he called her several times before leaving Kathmandu. She was in Spain, making a film. During his two weeks in the mountains, while getting acclimated to the altitude, he made two trips out to a phone to call her. Since crossing the Himalayas, he of course has been incommunicado."

Oztrak sought possible hidden meanings behind those phone calls. He found none. Naturally a man would call his wife when possible under those circumstances.

"Everything available on the man is there," Ramcek said, thumping the dossier with the flat of his hand. "I guarantee it."

Chang entered the discussion for the first time since Ramcek began his summation.

"I've also taken the trouble to consult with our diplomatic services. From their reports, and from what Ramcek has learned, we have concluded that this Loomis is not in Tibet on a mission for the CIA. Beijing has decided that at the moment a diplomatic protest to the Americans would not be in our best interest. In fact, Beijing has ruled out even any acknowledgment that we're aware an American citizen has entered Tibet illegally, for nefarious purposes. We prefer that the matter be disposed of quietly. So if you can take care of this problem for us, without attracting notice, we will be most grateful."

Oztrak had been wondering how to broach the subject of approval for his invasion. He recognized that approval had just been granted.

"You can rest assured that Loomis will be eliminated, Mr. Commissar."

Chang spoke softly, as if to lessen the impact of his words. "This Loomis has outwitted and outfought your men thus far. How can you be so sure you can defeat him this time?"

Oztrak chose his words with care. "I don't yet know what happened to Pishan in the pass. But Gungor was careless. I won't be."

"How many men are you taking into Tibet?"

Oztrak again felt the need for caution. In truth, he had not yet made that decision. If he took all of his men, the Red Chinese might grow concerned over such an army operating within their borders. On the other hand, he wanted to operate from a position of strength.

He sidestepped the question, hoping Chang would give him some indication of what was possible.

"I haven't yet set a number, Mr. Commissar. I'm keenly aware of the political implications."

"How many men do you have available?" Chang asked.

Oztrak was certain Chang knew the answer. "I have fifteen hundred young men committed to the *jihad.* Of these, roughly one thousand are trained sufficiently to be taken into the field."

Chang's analytical gaze rested on Oztrak for a long moment. "I believe you should go in force. Perhaps you won't need your entire army to do away with an American, an Englishman, and three hundred and fifty monks. But if you march through western Tibet attacking *all* Buddhists, a screen will be thrown over any assessment that Loomis and Lhalde are your primary targets."

Oztrak could hardly believe his good fortune. He had been granted approval to take his army into Tibet and to carry out his *jihad* without his even having to ask.

He wanted to be certain he had heard correctly.

"Beijing won't object?"

Chang's eyes narrowed, and for a moment Oztrak thought he almost smiled. "Let's regard this situation from the perspective of the people in Beijing. Tibet currently is in a state of rebellion. Most of this resistance is centered around the Buddhist elements. Beijing received worldwide condemnation for the use of force in the Tiananmen Square incident. If the government were to send its army into western Tibet to suppress the Buddhists, and word was leaked to the outside world, there would be repercussions. Protests in the United

Nations. Economic sanctions we can ill afford. But if an independent army of Muslims were to march through the region on a *jihad* and do this work on their own, Beijing's hands would be clean. Do you see the reasoning?"

Oztrak did. He was being given carte blanche.

"I will march into Tibet with a thousand men," he promised.

"I have only one caveat," Chang added. "Stop Loomis and do it quietly. With his wife so well known, his participation in this could cause untold complications. It would be to our advantage if he were simply to disappear from the face of the earth."

"You can rest assured, Mr. Commissar. He will be eliminated."

"I believe we understand each other," Chang said. "Officially, this conversation never took place. But I promise you: if you do your work well, and the problem of Loomis quietly goes away, Beijing will be most obligated to you. Your service in this matter will be rewarded."

Oztrak walked his visitors to the front door. He then returned to the packet of materials Ramcek had left. He spent the better part of an hour poring over them.

As Ramcek had said, all of the facts were there. Names, dates, places. Yet Ramcek sensed that the key element was missing. What motivated this man Loomis to travel halfway around the world to help a doomed lamasery?

Oztrak could not find the answer.

Turning back through the material, he picked up the small photograph. In it Loomis was surrounded by what appeared to be Filipino guerrillas. Oztrak rummaged in his desk, found a magnifying glass, and studied the picture.

Loomis was a big American, with a big American face. He had been photographed full-on, staring at the camera without any expression that Oztrak could discern. Oztrak sat examining the photograph for several minutes.

At last, restless, he walked to the end of the room and the sliding glass doors.

His children again were in the garden, in another session of play accorded them during their school day. His two oldest living sons had returned to their battle with the wooden swords. Oztrak slid open the glass door and went out. His children gathered around him.

He knelt on one knee and for a time coached his sons in their swordsmanship. He had always regretted that the art had passed from warfare. In his more reflective moments, he yearned for the days when his ancestors had laid waste with muscle and blade. In Oztrak's view that had been warfare at its elemental best. Today any coward could cock and aim a rifle. Only with the blade could a man cleave flesh and spill blood with his own daring and brawn.

The play period ended. Oztrak did not want to keep his children from their studies. He let them go and returned to his information packet.

Again he went over all of the material. He found nothing new. He returned to the photograph and examined it even more carefully. On this closer inspection, he thought he could discern undeniable intelligence and strength in the man's eyes. He sensed solid resolution in the set of the mouth.

As he studied the photograph, the feeling swept over him that the man seemed disturbingly familiar. Oztrak wondered if he had seen the man somewhere. But he dismissed the thought. The possibility was remote. His experience with Americans was limited. If ever he had met Loomis, surely he would remember.

Yet he could not shake the impression that they had encountered each other somewhere.

An hour later, he dined alone, taking his time, savoring the food. Tomorrow he would be returning to camp. Weeks might pass before he again would enjoy the comforts of home.

In early evening he went in to his new young wife. Although they had now been married seven years, he still thought of her as new, for he had lived twenty-six years with his first wife before she died in childbirth. He thought of his new wife as young, for his eldest daughter by his first wife was five years older. And his new young wife was beautiful, with a full, ruby-red mouth, laughing brown eyes, and hips as supple as a yearling mare.

Oztrak made love leisurely throughout the evening, satiating himself against the lonely nights he soon would know on the high plateau. He planted his seed deep, praying to Allah for another son.

He found comfort in the fact that not all duties of the *jihad* were grim.

Oztrak stood in the stirrups and rode ramrod straight. To his left Erek kept pace as they passed rank on rank of mounted Uighurs. Oztrak's saddle, lined with sheepskin in the ancient style, felt good against his thighs and buttocks. His horse, selected by Erek from a herd of two thousand, moved along at an effortless, easy trot.

The men of his squadrons appeared fit. As Oztrak rode past them, he carefully examined faces, bearing, rifles, equipment. Beards, colorful guidons rippled in the breeze. But the horses stood fast.

Oztrak and Erek reached the last squadron and Oztrak's inspection was completed. Abruptly he wheeled his horse to the right and rode a hundred meters away from the formation. Erek expertly kept on his left. Again Oztrak turned, and rode until he was in the middle of the drill field. There he stopped and faced his men.

Erek rode forward and shouted orders to the squadron commanders, who repeated them in perfect military fashion. The band began to play a traditional Uighur march. The cavalry formed eight abreast, moving at a brisk walk. Dressing right as they wheeled, the squadrons made two left turns and came down the field in review, passing within twenty meters of Oztrak.

As guidons dipped in his honor, Oztrak sat monitoring the quality of the horses and the skill of the riders, taking immense pleasure in the martial air of the band, the rhythm of the shouted orders, the drumming of horse hooves.

The review ended as the squadrons returned to formation. Oztrak was prepared to give the order to dismiss. But Erek presented a surprise.

For twenty minutes various riders performed feats of remarkable horsemanship while their comrades cheered. Some dashed across the field standing in the saddle. Others did handstands, and some tumbled in and out of the saddle, using their velocity to vault from one side of the horse to the other. It was an impressive demonstration of riding skills. Oztrak was left invigorated. This was soldiering as it once had been, centuries ago, when his ancestors first came into this region to clear it of nonbelievers.

After the formations were dismissed, Oztrak summoned Erek into his tent.

"You have done well," he said quietly. "The squadrons appear to be in superb condition."

"I've reorganized the men according to ability and training," Erek said. "But I haven't yet made a final disposition of officers, for I didn't know how many men you plan to take onto the high plateau."

"Ten squadrons," Oztrak said.

Erek could not keep his amazement out of his voice. "A thousand men?"

"Perhaps all won't be needed, but it'll be further training for them," Oztrak pointed out. "We'll move rapidly, destroy the lamasery, and make a sweep back through western Tibet. We'll be back here within twenty days. It will be the first of many such victories for Allah. As our movement spreads, we'll be needing experienced men and officers. This invasion will give us an ample supply."

At sunset the squadrons again came onto the field, this time without horses but with prayer rugs. Fifteen hundred strong, Oztrak's command bowed in the direction of Mecca. Prostrate, foreheads to the ground, the men rededicated themselves to the *jihad.*

It was an emotional moment, and Oztrak was deeply affected. For a time he had difficulty keeping his voice under control.

Afterward, he summoned his squadron commanders to his tent and faced them under the light of burning flares.

"You have prepared well," he said. "Now you shall be rewarded. Tomorrow at dawn we will leave with a thousand men for the high plateau to destroy the lamasery of the Kamala Lama. And this I promise you on the pain of death: you shall have a victory."

11

Loomis walked down the firing line, carefully studying the posture of each of his warrior monks. They had practiced with the Kalashnikovs to the point of familiarity. But they were still far from acquiring expertise with the weapons. Loomis knew he had to accept certain limitations. He had neither time nor sufficient ammunition to turn the warrior monks into sharpshooters.

He watched the ten-man squad dry-firing at cardboard silhouettes erected on the ridge to the right of the lamasery entrance. Thus far they had not fired live rounds. Loomis planned to allocate a half clip to each man in final practice. With no more training than that, they would face the enemy.

Loomis had encountered little difficulty in training them on posture and on how to hold the rifle. Walking down the firing line, he noted with satisfaction that their prone positions were almost perfect and their concentration on the target was exceptional. Most held their rifles steady. Not a single rifle barrel wavered.

The warrior monks clearly made a fetish of keeping in good physical shape. That was a plus. Most were comparatively young, which also helped. Perhaps because of their many hours spent in meditation, all seemed slow and deliberate in their movements. Loomis long had observed that this type of men often made good soldiers —if they were not *too* slow.

Loomis looked out across the plain into the distance, where he expected first sighting of the enemy. The sun was bright, the day clear. The landscape was so vast and the detail so sharp that momentary pain shot through his eyes. He raised a hand to ward off the glare and searched carefully.

Nothing moved on that barren stretch of grassland.

He turned and walked back down the firing line to where Owenby and Khedru stood waiting.

"They're showing improvement," he said to Owenby. "But I'm still concerned that when the time comes they won't shoot to kill. Tell Khedru that."

Owenby translated and received a lengthy reply from Khedru.

"He says they'll kill if necessary."

"That's exactly it," Loomis said. "They've got to understand going in that it'll be necessary. We can't waste a single bullet. Tell him that."

As Owenby translated, Khedru frowned, revealing his discomfiture with the thought. His sorrowful eyes glanced from Owenby to Loomis and back again as he listened.

Above them, up on the ridges, other monks were at work digging and erecting the defenses. Loomis glanced up to the mountaintop, to make certain the lookouts were still on station and alert. From the peak, with binoculars, the lookouts could spot movement up to forty or fifty miles away. With signal mirrors, they would report on number, speed, and direction.

Owenby listened to Khedru's lengthy reply. He waited until the end before translating for Loomis.

"He's giving us a jolly bunch of shit. It's full of their

Buddhist mumbo jumbo, but in essence he says they all have vowed to kill if it's vitally necessary to protect the Kamala Lama."

Khedru stood looking at Loomis, obviously expecting some sort of approval. Loomis did not answer. He stood watching the men dry-firing.

On the previous evening the warrior monks had given Loomis a complete demonstration of their ability to maim and disable an opponent with staves or, if required, with their bare hands. Clearly they had expected him to be impressed, and to some extent he had been. They were an unusually athletic group of young men, and they had honed their skills admirably. But the demonstration had left Loomis deeply disturbed. It had confirmed his first impression that the warrior monks did not have a single lethal blow in their repertoire.

"Tell Khedru to bring all his monks down here," Loomis ordered.

Within minutes the fifty warrior monks were assembled. Loomis gestured for them to sit on the grass. He stood facing them.

"Get my words across to them as accurately as you can," Loomis told Owenby.

The monks sat looking up at him, their curiosity obvious. As Loomis talked, he watched their faces, evaluating their reaction.

"I understand you men have vowed to kill in defense of the Kamala Lama, *if necessary.* What I am telling you now is that if this lamasery is attacked, you *must* kill." He pointed. "When the Uighur Muslims come riding across that plain toward us, shooting, there'll be no time for you to make your decision. You must make it now."

Loomis paused, allowing time for translation, and for the monks to absorb his words. He lowered his voice to a more confidential tone.

"If you feel you can't kill with the first bullet you fire, we'll give your gun to someone who can. We must make full use of every gun. If you have any doubts whatsoever on your ability to kill when the time comes, report to

Owenby or to Khedru. We'll find a place for you to serve elsewhere, and no stigma will be attached. I recognize that this is a moral decision. Every man must make it for himself. But it is one that must be made, and made now."

Loomis had no doubt that his talk hit home. Every set of eyes looking up at him grew troubled. But not a single man spoke.

"Let's get back to practice," Loomis concluded. "While the next squad works with the targets, I want the rest of you to watch and listen. Pay careful attention, so that when your turn comes, you won't make the same mistakes."

He worked them hard through the afternoon, reviewing the loading and firing procedures, getting them accustomed to placing the sights on the silhouette of a man and squeezing the trigger.

Not a single man approached Owenby or Khedru to express qualms over killing.

Loomis had no inkling as to what was in their minds. He hoped that Owenby, with some knowledge of the language, might have received some indication.

"What do you think?" Loomis asked.

"I told you two days ago, old sod. I think you and I should be on our jolly way back to Kathmandu."

Loomis persisted. "Will they shoot to kill?"

"Really, I haven't the balmiest. I think they're still chewing on that fiery speech you gave them. But I suspect that at this point they really don't know themselves."

Loomis and Owenby climbed over the ridge, laboring with the altitude. Originally the lamasery's two munitions experts, Rinpang and Drupa, had set up their factory inside the cave. But Loomis had convinced them of the folly. Now they had set up shop in the next valley.

Loomis reached the top of the ridge and stopped to catch his breath. Owenby came up beside him and sank onto the grass, breathing hard. Loomis looked back.

More than a hundred monks were hard at work along

the ridges, digging trenches and barricades. No longer would the entrance to the lamasery be difficult to find. From the distance, it now resembled a giant badger hole, with mounds of fresh dirt glaringly in evidence.

The wind had been high earlier in the day, but now had died down to a gentle breeze. Loomis walked a few paces further and peered into the next valley.

The munitions factory was in full operation. Over the years, Rinpang and Drupa had trained two dozen or more monks. Now they were at work in a series of lean-to shelters, each a step in an assembly line. In theory, each shelter was far enough from the others that a single accident would not endanger the rest.

Owenby was still lying on the grass.

"Let's go," Loomis said. "It's all downhill from here."

"That doesn't cheer me in the least," Owenby said. "I'm already dreading the bloody climb back."

Loomis and Owenby made their way down the side of the ridge. As they approached, Drupa looked up from his work and called out to them.

"He says they worked all night and doubled the pile of gunpowder they had yesterday," Owenby translated. "If that's true, they ought to have enough to blow up the whole bloody mountain."

The munitions factory was the one area that had given Loomis little difficulty. The monks were turning out gunpowder at a surprising rate, and the quality was unexpectedly high.

The formula, gleaned from old Chinese manuscripts, utilized only the basics: sulfur, saltpeter, and charcoal. Anticipating years of tunneling, the monks had assembled a large supply of each. But the work had gone so fast that the manufacturing exceeded the supply. Now old shelving, tables, every scrap of wood available had been utilized for charcoal. Sheep dung was yielding the nitrates for saltpeter. Bags of sulfur had been brought in from mineral springs at a lake thirty kilometers distant. Utilizing their ancient Chinese formulas, the monks were cooking and drying their deadly brew.

"Ask him if the test rockets are ready," Loomis said.

On Owenby's question, Drupa smiled and led them a quarter of a mile away from the shelters to a stack of completed munitions.

Three test rockets lay in their launching cradles. Each was eight feet long, resembling an oversized Roman candle.

Loomis had yet to determine how effective the rockets would be as weapons.

In his early planning, Loomis had scoured the lamasery for any kind of pipe that might be used. He had found nothing. It had been Zampo, the ancient librarian, who had remembered the lengths of bamboo used to carry goods onto the high plateau back in the early fifties. Long unused, the bamboo shafts had been stored in the back of the library, ready to be put into service if ever again the lamasery was forced to move.

The wood was not strong enough for use alone. But firmly wrapped with rawhide cord, it could contain considerable pressures. The gunpowder was slow-burning, perfect for rocketry. Early experiments had proved successful. Loomis had fired the first three more than a half mile. Now he needed to figure angle and distance.

Drupa spoke to Owenby for several minutes, gesturing toward the sky, the plain.

"He says Zampo found an old manuscript that describes how the Chinese aimed their rockets back in the sixth century," Owenby translated. "The speed and rate of climb for his rockets may be different, he says, but the principle will probably be the same."

Loomis and Owenby waited while Drupa painstakingly adjusted the first rocket. He was a small, wiry little man with a thick gray thatch around his perfectly bald head. He reminded Loomis of one of the characters in *Snow White and the Seven Dwarfs,* but he could not remember which.

Drupa began an explanation of his adjustments. Owenby translated.

"He says this one is aimed precisely at forty-five degrees. It should travel on a trajectory like this."

Drupa—or perhaps Zampo—had made a drawing. Loomis gave it close examination, imagining the effect.

"Okay, let's try it," Loomis said.

Drupa lit the fuse. The rocket shot off its cradle and went high—too high—before beginning its descent. The ingenious warhead Drupa had devised—a metal can filled with gunpowder—exploded harmlessly at least sixty feet in the air.

"Tell him the trajectory needs to be lower," Loomis said.

After discussion, Drupa settled on an angle of thirty-five degrees. He adjusted the second rocket and lit the fuse.

It sped in a perfect arc, hitting the ground a hundred and fifty yards away. But the warhead exploded too late, a full second after the rocket struck the ground.

Talking animatedly, Drupa moved to the third rocket.

"He says he can shorten the internal fuse between the propellant and the warhead," Owenby translated. "This rocket should travel the same course, but the warhead will explode before it hits."

Carefully, Drupa cut a length off the fuse and reinserted it into the warhead. He adjusted the angle of the rocket and lit the fuse.

The third bamboo shaft traversed the same arc. True to Drupa's estimate, the warhead exploded about ten feet off the ground.

"Bloody well perfect," Owenby said. "Pity it's nothing but a noisemaker."

"Maybe it'll do the job," Loomis said.

They returned to the lean-to shelters. There Loomis examined the crude claymores he had devised and the monks had put into production.

Short lengths of bamboo had been stuffed with gunpowder and bits of metal in emulation of a shotgun shell. Loomis hoped that with them arranged in clusters, they would be deadly at short range. Using the primers from precious ammunition, he had made small detonators that would light the fuses that would fire the claymores. By using a rawhide cord, the devices could be fired from some distance away.

His attempt at land mines had been less successful. He had been unable to find suitable containers. The iron pots from the kitchen were too brittle. Eventually all the pots had been broken up by the blacksmith for use in the claymores.

But in his hand grenades Loomis had been far more successful. Each was created from a short length of bamboo wrapped with rawhide cord and studded with jagged metal. With fuses of various measured lengths, the grenades promised to be one of the most valuable weapons in his arsenal.

Since they had only thirty Kalashnikovs, twenty of the fifty warrior monks were left without effective weapons. Loomis had put them to work practicing the art of throwing the foot-long sticks. Each grenadier was assigned an assistant, who would light the fuse just before the grenade was thrown.

The stacks of rockets, claymores, and grenades were growing rapidly. Loomis was amazed over the amount of gunpowder the monks had produced in such a short time. Satisfied that all was going well in his munitions factory, he led Owenby back over the ridge to the lamasery entrance.

The half-excavated entrenchments were deserted. The monks were filing back into the lamasery.

Loomis was appalled. After four days of work, the defenses were not yet half completed. Yet the monks were walking off the job.

"What the hell are they doing?" Loomis asked.

"Going back to their meditation and their bloody prayer wheels, I suppose," Owenby said.

Loomis was furious. No one seemed to understand the seriousness of the situation.

"Let's go find Lhalde," he said.

He led Owenby inside. After a search, they located

Lhalde. He sat in a room with two score other monks, eyes closed, lips moving ceaselessly. Loomis and Owenby stood in the corridor and waited.

"Way things are going, maybe we'd best go in and join in the prayers," Owenby said.

Loomis did not answer. With all the work and contingency planning yet to be done, Lhalde and his monks were wasting half of every day.

At last Lhalde opened his eyes. When he saw Loomis and Owenby waiting in the corridor, he rose and came out to them.

"We've got to talk," Loomis told him. "Where can we go?"

"This way," Lhalde said.

He took them into a small room heavy with incense. Loomis ignored an invitation to sit. He did not mince words.

"We have only a slim chance of saving this lamasery, even if everyone here works around the clock. Right now there's two hours of sun out there going to waste. The trenches and barricades are only half completed. We can't afford to lose the time. Something must be done."

Lhalde's calm, self-possessed demeanor did not waver. "We of the lamasery have certain duties, certain vows to perform. We have *vinaya*—a system of monastic discipline. It must be preserved. It takes precedence above all else."

"Even above life itself?"

Lhalde met his gaze. "Yes."

"Loomis, I told you," Owenby said. "It's a lost cause."

"I respectfully request to see the Kamala Lama," Loomis said.

Lhalde's hesitation was brief. "I'll take you to him."

Again they walked down dim, narrow corridors and descended the flight of steps into the private quarters of the Kamala Lama. Lhalde motioned for Loomis and Owenby to wait. He stepped through the curtained door, talked briefly with the lama in Tibetan, then motioned for Loomis and Owenby to enter.

The lama sat ensconced on his red and gold pillows. Loomis, Owenby, and Lhalde stood facing him.

"Mr. Loomis believes all religious duties of the lamasery should be suspended during this crisis," Lhalde explained. "I feel that under the circumstances adherence to *vinaya* should be observed now more than ever. So we have come to you, my spiritual master, to seek your wisdom."

The lama looked up at Loomis with his boyish face. He contemplated the problem in silence for the better part of a minute.

"You are both wise men. I can only conclude that you both are correct. Mr. Loomis should have the physical services of anyone and everyone in the lamasery for as many hours each day as he wishes. And you, Lhalde, are correct in that the monks must not abandon their vows and religious obligations. So I propose that the monks continue their work and that they say their mantras and prayers while performing that work."

Loomis could find no objection to that. Neither, apparently, could Lhalde.

"I urge you both to continue with all possible speed," the lama added. "I'm convinced an attack will come soon."

"How soon?" Loomis asked, thinking of all the work yet to be done.

The lama closed his eyes and did not speak for a long interval. But at last he opened his eyes.

"I'm not certain," he said. "But I sense it will be *very* soon."

The words of the Kamala Lama were disseminated and the lamasery went into a frenzy of preparation. The monks worked long hours, and at last the trenches and barricades in front of the entrance and along the two ridges were completed. The woven grass screens were finished and installed, partially hiding the excavations.

Throughout the week of frantic work Loomis and

Owenby hardly slept. They drilled the monks until each man knew exactly what was expected of him.

In the evenings Loomis met repeatedly with Lhalde and the Kamala Lama, mapping out contingency plans in case the defenses failed.

At last came the morning when the lookouts signaled excitedly from the mountaintop. The report was sobering: a large body of mounted men, forty miles away, moving straight toward the lamasery mountain.

"How many?" Loomis asked.

His query was sent up and the answer came back: still too far away to count, but many, many men.

Two hours later an estimate was signaled down from the peak: hundreds upon hundreds. Perhaps one thousand men.

"Surely the bloody chaps exaggerate," Owenby said. "Why would the Uighurs send a brigade to do the work of a platoon?"

"Direction?" Loomis asked.

The word came back: the mounted men were still coming direct to the lamasery.

Loomis looked at the sun, low on the western horizon. "They won't get here until just before dark," he said. "I doubt they'll try a night attack."

He felt he had to know more. Leaving the ridge, he labored up the side of the mountain until he could see the approaching Uighurs.

The lookouts had not exaggerated. The column of troops was wide and yet stretched out for a half mile. They came on relentlessly, raising a heavy plume of dust.

Loomis was dismayed. Despite all the talk of a thousand, perhaps fifteen hundred Uighurs committed to the *jihad,* he had expected to be attacked by no more than three or four hundred. As Owenby had said, why send a brigade to do the work of a platoon?

But he was committed. No retreat was possible. With only thirty rifles, fifty untested fighting men, and explosives made from centuries-old formulas, he must defend the lamasery against an army of a thousand well-trained troops.

He hurried back to the ridge. But as he had predicted, the Uighurs delayed their attack. They erected their tents out on the plain, well within sight of the monks and their paltry defenses, to await the following dawn.

Loomis was making a final tour of the barricades when Lhalde found him.

"If you can spare a moment, the Kamala Lama desires to see you," Lhalde said. "He asked me to tell you that it is important."

"Is there any hope of saving the lamasery?" the Kamala Lama asked.

Loomis sat uncomfortably on red-and-gold pillows facing the lama in his private quarters. Lhalde had withdrawn, leaving them alone. The lama sat in his relaxed lotus position, smiling slightly, awaiting Loomis's answer.

Loomis saw no reason to hedge. "If we're lucky, we may be able to hold them off for a day or so. But eventually we'll be worn down by sheer numbers."

"Then the lamasery will fall?"

"It's almost inevitable," Loomis said.

The lama closed his eyes for a moment. He opened them and regarded Loomis solemnly.

"Never before have I so sensed the presence of evil as I do tonight," he said. "In your Western cultures, your Western religions you have all but eliminated belief in the evil forces abroad in the world. But we in the East, with cultures and religions of a more contemplative nature, have never forgotten that evil is a constant presence, forever attempting to erase whatever good we do."

Loomis had no quarrel with that. He waited. The scent of incense hung heavily in the lama's small chamber. Flickering tapers lit the room dimly. From the library next door came faint sounds as the monks made preparations for the battle and possible aftermath.

"We in Tibet have become intimately acquainted with the forces of evil during the last four decades," the lama continued. "Our government in exile now estimates that one million, two hundred thousand Tibetans have been slaughtered since the Communists first occupied our country at midcentury. This in a nation with a population of less than six million. One in five of our countrymen slain. Three thousand, five hundred lamaseries destroyed. Hundreds of thousands of monks defrocked. Most of them slain. Six thousand temples destroyed. I must ask myself, How long can we continue to adhere to our policy of nonviolence? What profits us to persist in turning the other cheek?"

Loomis remained silent. The lama again closed his eyes for a time. When he opened them, he smiled.

"While learning English, I happened onto American Westerns, the majority by the author Frederick Faust, who wrote under the nom de plume Max Brand. Are you familiar with him?"

Loomis nodded. "He also wrote the Dr. Kildare series."

"And many, many other novels. More than four hundred, I'm told. Wondrous, gripping stories. Mr. Faust once said something that fascinated me. He said all his books have the same basic plot: A good man turns bad to make the bad man good."

"A plot from life itself," Loomis said.

"Correct you are," the lama said. "But, you see, when the good man turns bad to make the bad man good, then you emerge with two bad men. Evil has prevailed."

Loomis disagreed. "If the good man has done his work well, you'll be left with two good men."

"Perhaps," the lama said. "But if so, they are good men who have practiced evil. Good hasn't prevailed throughout."

Loomis nodded to acknowledge the point.

"Which brings me to my present quandary," the lama continued. "Shall I sit back and do nothing while my fifty monk warriors turn bad in order to make the bad men good? Can I remain above the fray? Of course, the answer is no. I can't. Not in good conscience. I must share with them this venture into evil."

Again Loomis remained silent.

"I have told my warrior monks I wish to speak with them. Please be seated at my right hand and bear witness to what I tell them."

Loomis moved to the cushions on the lama's right. The lama picked up a small bell at his feet and gave it a perfunctory shake. The fifty warrior monks filed into the small room, bowed to the lama, and seated themselves. Hardly an inch of floor space was left. Yet somehow Lhalde walked through them to sit beside Loomis.

The lama glanced at Loomis. "Lhalde will translate my words for you."

After a long pause, he began to speak. The words were melodic, repetitious.

"He is reciting an ancient Buddhist mantra, asking God's wisdom in our earthly acts," Lhalde whispered.

The mantra was repeated by the warrior monks. For many minutes the rhythmic cadence of the chanting filled the room. The flickering tapers, the closeness of the room cast an eerie spell over the ceremony. After a time the chanting ended abruptly.

In the silence that followed the Kamala Lama raised his hands palm outward in an attitude of blessing. He held them there while he resumed speaking. Lhalde waited until a pause before conveying a summary to Loomis.

"He has told them that the lamasery is besieged by our ancient enemies. He said it is doubtful our defense will succeed in saving the lamasery."

Loomis carefully studied the faces of the warrior monks. Apparently the Kamala Lama was not telling them anything they did not know.

But with the lama's next long discourse, the atmosphere gradually changed. The warrior monks were clearly shocked by what they heard. Several raised their voices in protest.

Lhalde leaned close to Loomis. "The Holy Lama told them he understands if some among them harbor doubts on their ability to kill when the time comes. He said the karma of killing is terrible to contemplate and that he wishes to lift some of that burden from them. Therefore he is ordering them to kill in order to take the full weight of the karma upon himself."

Khedru spoke for a time, and several of his monks made sounds of agreement.

"Khedru is begging the Holy Lama not to do this," Lhalde translated. "He said the warriors have talked among themselves and that all have agreed that killing will be necessary. He said not one among them will fail in his duty."

The Kamala Lama gave Khedru a brief reply.

"The Holy Lama stated that it is *his* duty to take the responsibility, and the penalties, for what must be done. He said he will now bless them, each and every one."

Loomis sat motionless while the warriors came forward, one by one, to kneel at the lama's feet. The lama took each head in both hands, closed his eyes, and apparently said a silent prayer.

Several of the monks left the room in tears after receiving their blessing. All seemed devastated.

Khalde motioned to Loomis and led him out of the room into the corridor. He also seemed shaken.

"I hope you understand what this means," Khalde said. "We long have known that our Holy One is close to nirvana. Through many incarnations he has risen to a state of such perfection that his soul is near its union with the supreme being. Tonight, by ordering his monks to kill, taking the burden of karma on himself, he has regressed several incarnations in his upward spiral."

Loomis did not answer. But he understood. He remembered the lama's earlier rambling discourse. An exceedingly good man had just turned bad in an effort to make some exceptionally bad men good.

12

The moon had long since set and darkness lay over the mountains. Yet dawn was not far away. Already a thin, almost imperceptible band of light stretched across the eastern horizon. A soft breeze blew from the south. Although the temperatures had fallen into the lower teens during the night, Loomis was confident the rising sun would soon provide a comparatively warm day.

Stretched full-length in the grass on the right-hand ridge, Loomis raised his binoculars and studied the dim red pinpoints of light on the plain. He could not yet see enough detail to make out what was happening. But apparently the Uighurs were cooking their breakfast.

Owenby came to sprawl beside him.

"I just walked the length of the other ridge," Owenby said. "Everyone's in place. We're as ready as we'll ever be."

"What shape are they in mentally?" Loomis asked.

"With these people, who the hell knows? They could be scared shitless and still give you that blank look."

"You tell them to stay hidden?"

"Twenty fucking times."

Loomis was worried about discipline. Keeping under cover during an all-out cavalry charge would be difficult enough for experienced, battle-hardened soldiers. Yet if a single man panicked, the essential element of surprise would be lost.

The light in the east was spreading rapidly. Loomis glanced behind him. The mountain, the ridges were assuming form. Overhead, the stars were growing pale.

"This bloody waiting is what gets me," Owenby said.

"It won't be a long wait," Loomis said. "He'll try to take advantage of the sun hitting us in the eyes. We can expect him to attack within the hour after sunup."

Owenby gave Loomis a sidelong glance in the semi-darkness. *"Him?* You know the bastard?"

With that question Loomis realized that he indeed had been thinking in terms of a personified enemy. He thought of the Kamala Lama's theory of battles in previous lives, refought in the new between the same adversaries.

He was uncomfortable with the thought, but he felt he truly knew the man in command out there, whatever his name.

"I'm assuming it is the fellow you heard rumors about," Loomis said. "The Muslim leader. What was his name?"

"Oztrak," Owenby said. "But I doubt it's him. The way I heard it he's the big cheese in those parts. Leading the holy war, playing footsie with the Chinese. I wouldn't think he'd come all this way himself, just to wipe out a small lamasery."

Again Loomis raised his binoculars. With the growing light, details were becoming more distinct. He now could see men milling around the fires out on the plain. Horses were being brought in and saddled. The size of the Uighur army was sobering. With the many tents and all of the activity, the encampment resembled a small city.

Loomis turned his binoculars on the opposite ridge. The monks had done a superb job of hiding the entrenchments. Grass screens lay across the raw earth. Slowly Loomis examined the entire ridge. He did not see a single man. All were well hidden.

No evidence of preparation was evident except the large entrenchment directly in front of, and slightly below, the entrance to the lamasery. With any luck, the enemy would assume that to be the sole defense and concentrate his attack there.

"Something's happening," Owenby said.

Again Loomis focused his binoculars on the encampment. Owenby was right. Already the horses were saddled. They were being led into some semblance of formation.

"Better get back to your post," Loomis said. "I think he'll come at us on first good light."

"Right-o," Owenby said. He eased out of the slit trench, then paused. "You want to know something, old sod? Maybe I'm losing my fucking mind, but I'm not as frightened as I thought I would be. I'm scared. But I'm still functioning."

"When it starts, you'll be too busy to worry about it," Loomis told him. "Just think of the job ahead of us. You'll do fine."

Owenby trotted away, hunkered down to present a low profile. Despite doubts, Loomis had placed him in charge of the defenses on the opposite ridge. Khedru commanded the small force behind the entrenchments directly in front of the lamasery entrance.

Loomis resumed his watch on the enemy encampment. Rosy shafts of light now filled the eastern sky. Behind him, all darkness had lifted.

Out on the grassy plain, the cavalry units were taking shape, spread over a quarter of a mile. He counted ten squadrons. Each appeared to consist of about a hundred men.

Now certainty replaced any doubt: The lamasery's fifty warrior monks faced an army of more than one thousand trained cavalrymen. It was a disparity in numbers reminiscent of Thermopylae and the Alamo. But here in this remote corner of the world, the warrior monks could die heroically and no one would ever know.

Loomis felt the old, familiar uneasiness rising in his groin. He had fought in many battles. Always it was the same. Not fear, exactly. But the exhilaration that came with placing one's life on the line, of knowing that this might be the day the odds at last evened out.

He had been in such tight situations before, outnumbered, with back to the wall. But in every instance he at least had the support of well-trained troops. Today he had only thirty riflemen who had yet to fire full clips through their weapons and twenty grenadiers armed only with jerry-rigged bamboo-and-scrap-metal devices. And Owenby had been right: The rockets were no more than noisemakers.

The rim of the sun came over the horizon, flooding the plain with yellow light. From the plain came the distinctive notes of a bugle. Loomis at first assumed it a call for the Uighurs to mount their horses. But to his surprise, the thousand men bowed in unison, then prostrated themselves upon the ground. All were facing in the same direction. On the clear air, Loomis could hear the voice of the imam leading the prayer.

The ceremony made Loomis fully aware, for the first time, that he was caught up in a war of religion—between two faiths each believing it had the answers. The only difficulty was that one was militant and the other was not.

With the morning sun, the southern breeze increased, sending waves across the knee-high grass on the plain. Loomis put aside his binoculars and made last-minute preparations.

The signal rocket—a primitive Roman candle—lay at his feet. He pushed its support into the ground so that the rocket would arc over his own men. He took out his .380 Belgian automatic and placed it on the parapet in front of him. He glanced behind him. His riflemen lay flat in their slit trenches, awaiting the signal. Farther back, near the entrance to the lamasery, the riflemen serving as bait had taken up their positions.

Their entrenchment, nestled into the juncture of the two ridges, seemed frail and ineffective. Loomis wondered if the enemy would take the bait, never suspecting a trap.

Blood-chilling yells came from the enemy encampment. Loomis reached for his binoculars.

The religious ceremony had ended. The Uighurs were on their feet, waving their rifles, working themselves into a frenzy with an enormous pep rally.

The shouting continued several minutes. As the noise at last died away, again the bugle sounded.

Almost as a single man, the Uighurs climbed into their saddles. Again the blood-chilling yells erupted. But this time the shouting was of a shorter duration. In response to a series of bugle calls, the squadrons maneuvered into position.

From the military precision Loomis could see that the cavalry units were well trained. Each time the squadrons wheeled into a new formation, guidon bearers dashed to take up their new positions. The enemy commander had laid his plans well.

Loomis lowered his binoculars for a moment. The rising sun was blinding. Fortunately, the sun might not be as much of an obstacle as the enemy commander believed.

Again came a series of bugle calls. The Uighur squadrons maneuvered into position for the charge. From what Loomis could discern, the Uighur commander was committing eight squadrons to the charge, holding two in reserve.

Slowly, the Uighur army moved forward at a walk. Eerily, a band struck up a martial air. The pace shifted to a trot.

Even in his depth of concern, Loomis found himself admiring the military precision of the advancing cavalry. Each troop came eight abreast. Only a slight interval separated the troops. Throughout the increasing speed of the charge, each rank remained perfectly dressed to the right.

The rhythm of hooves changed from a trot to a gallop. Loomis dropped lower behind the parapet. Four hundred yards away, on some means of command Loomis could not discern, the squadrons shifted into a full, all-out charge.

Shouting, waving their Mausers high, the squadrons swept into the notch between the ridges. Loomis held his breath. They seemed to be taking the bait, charging straight for the entrenchment in front of the lamasery entrance. The constant drumming of hooves rose to a ground-shaking roar.

Loomis risked a peek over the parapet as the first squadrons thundered by. The Uighurs wore thick sheepskin coats and leather trousers. Every man wore crossed bandoliers stuffed with cartridges. Leather caps—heavy as helmets—covered their heads. Every man was standing in the saddle, cocked to one side, aiming his rifle at the entrenchments ahead. They were led by a striking young man whose moustache and full beard rippled in the wind. With sword held high, he led the squadrons on down the valley toward the entrenchments.

The young leader brought his sword down. The leading elements of the charge fired a volley into the entrenchments from a distance of more than two hundred yards.

Loomis waited. He wanted more Uighurs to enter the trap. Not until the first squadrons were within seventy-five yards of the barricade did he light the fuse.

The rocket rose in a high arc. In an instant grass screens fell away on each side of the ridge. The warrior monks, safely ensconced in their slit trenches, opened fire. With satisfaction Loomis observed that the monk warriors were shooting to kill. He could tell from the way the Uighurs toppled from the saddle. Within seconds dozens were down, their well-trained horses continuing the charge with empty saddles.

A moment later, from behind the barricades came the

first rockets, crackling over the first troops to explode in the midst of those a hundred yards behind them. Loomis wondered how Drupa and his men managed to light so many fuses so quickly. The rockets came in a sustained barrage, with six or eight in the air constantly.

As Loomis had hoped, the horses panicked. No doubt trained to rifle fire, they were overwhelmed by the sight and sounds of rockets whistling close overhead. All over the valley floor horses reared, pitched, and milled out of control as they fought their bits.

On each side of the barricade and all along each ridge the claymores fired. Horses and men dropped.

Instinctively, many of the Uighurs pressed close to the ridges, attempting to get out of the line of fire. There they came within range of the grenadiers, who rained explosive bamboo sticks down upon them. Scores of Uighurs fell from their saddles, wounded.

Loomis was pleased to see that he had positioned his riflemen effectively. The Uighurs were caught in a deadly crossfire. Survivors in the trap, attempting to retreat, were bottled in by the squadrons in the rear, still attempting to move forward into the action.

But soon all momentum was lost. Squadrons not yet under fire hesitated, disconcerted by the slaughter. Riderless horses poured past them, racing out of the valley.

Still the deadly fire continued until hardly a Uighur was left in the saddle in the vicinity of the barricades.

From the rear of the column a bugle sounded. The remainder of the Uighurs wheeled their horses and retreated, leaving the ground littered with their dead and wounded.

Loomis left his slit trench and walked to the edge of the ridge. Already his special teams from among the grenadiers raced out to slit the throats of the wounded. Other monks, noncombatants, ran out onto the battlefield to seize weapons and ammunition. Many gathered three or four rifles and a load of bandoliers before running back to cover.

Making a quick visual survey of the battlefield below,

Loomis estimated that the Uighurs had lost more than two hundred men.

He walked up the ridge toward the entrance to the lamasery. In a slit trench, one of his riflemen was down, a neat bullet hole through his forehead. Three other warrior monks were kneeling beside the body. They looked up at Loomis without expression. Loomis shook his head in sympathy and walked on past them.

Owenby came running to meet him at the barricade. "We did it," he said, laughing. "We bloody well did it."

Loomis did not feel like celebrating. The bulk of his munitions had been used. All element of surprise was gone. They had won the first round. But the battle had just started, and the Uighurs still had almost eight hundred men at their disposal.

"Go find out how many men we lost," Loomis said. "Get a count on how many rockets, how many grenades we have left. How much ammo for the Kalashnikovs."

Owenby looked toward the Uighur encampment. "What'll the buggers do now?"

"They'll lick their wounds an hour or two," Loomis predicted. "That'll give us a little time to get ready. But they'll probably come at us again sometime today."

"Like before? Surely they won't try that again."

"No," Loomis agreed. "This time they'll try something different."

Oztrak led the way into his tent. Erek and the squadron commanders entered behind him. They stood awkwardly, ill-at-ease.

"Be seated," Oztrak ordered. "We must reconstruct what happened."

He could hardly contain his anger. He could hardly believe that two hundred and twenty-six of his men were dead and that his precious troops, trained and polished to perfection, had been defeated in their first pitched battle.

Yet he could not blame himself. Who would have expected a handful of warrior monks to lay down such deadly fire? How could he have anticipated rockets? Bamboo grenades? Shotgunlike devices that scattered metal pellets?

"Why did the assault fail?" he asked.

"We lost control of our horses because of the rockets," Erek said. "We were within reach of the barricade when it happened. The horses began pitching, rearing, shying away. The men could not aim their rifles and manage their horses at the same time."

Oztrak nodded. He had seen the difficulty from his vantage point with the headquarters company in the rear. He wanted to say words of comfort to Erek, who obviously was badly shaken by the experience. There, for a terrible moment, Oztrak had thought he saw Erek and his horse go down. He had been elated when Erek later rode out of the valley safely.

"It was the crossfire," Batu said. "The bullets came from every direction. There was no place to make a stand, to fight back. For the infidels, it must have been like shooting a lion in his cage."

Batu, a squadron commander, was wounded. Blood flowed freely from a puncture on his neck, but he refused treatment. He said it was only a cut, caused by a bit of metal from one of the grenades.

"We had no place to attack," said Guven, commander of the second squadron. "They were spread out all along each ridge. Down in their trenches, they were very small targets, especially for men fighting on horseback."

"The sides of the ridges are too steep for the horses," Batu added. "We are at a disadvantage."

"We must flank them," Erek said. "Get above them. Cut them off from the entrance to the lamasery. Put them in a trap of our own."

Oztrak nodded agreement. He was hard put to contain his pride in Erek. The youth was thinking well, despite his harrowing experience only minutes ago. Oztrak had been making plans along the same line.

"How would you do that?" Oztrak asked, hoping Erek

would distinguish himself by devising a plan on his own, thereby confirming his selection as second-in-command.

"I could take a handful of picked men up over the right-hand ridge. The imbecile said there is a trail that leads to the mouth of the cave. From that height we could fire down into the trenches while the rest of the command makes another charge. We would have the monks caught in a crossfire from above and from below."

"That might work," Oztrak said. "We could create a diversion by making a feint with a squadron or two of cavalry. Does anyone have any other suggestions?"

Batu glanced at the other squadron commanders before replying. "My commander, it occurs to me we are faced with a master tactician. Perhaps he will anticipate an approach over the ridge, since it is lacking in subtlety. He may have a trap set there, waiting."

Oztrak hesitated, wondering how much of Batu's opposition stemmed from jealousy of Erek.

"What would you advise?" he asked Batu.

Again Batu glanced at the other commanders. Oztrak knew then that the opposition to Erek was general among the squadron commanders. Apparently they had even talked about it among themselves.

"I would search for another entrance," Batu said. "One must exist somewhere."

"The imbecile said there was no other," Erek said. "He was questioned thoroughly on that point."

"Then how do they get air inside?" Batu asked. "How can more than three hundred men live underground without constantly receiving a supply of fresh air?"

Oztrak had never stopped to consider. He realized that Batu's point was valid.

"They may have drilled some air shafts," Erek said. "The openings could be anywhere on the mountain. It would take weeks to make a thorough search."

That was true. Oztrak felt he should end the argument.

"The imbecile was emphatic in his insistence that no other entrance exists. He didn't possess the mental capacity to lie. Erek is correct in his thinking. We don't have time to search for what may not exist."

Batu said no more. But a veil seemed to slide over the faces of the squadron commanders, rendering them expressionless. Oztrak felt their resentment, and that aroused his own anger.

How could the other commanders fail to see Erek's daring and brilliance? But Oztrak knew he could say nothing to help. Erek must win their confidence himself.

"Then it is decided," he said. "Erek will take an assault force up the face of the mountain and over the right-hand ridge. The squadrons will feint an attack. Then, when Erek signals from the mountain, we will make a combined, all-out assault."

"We have eight dead, twelve wounded," Owenby said. "Six of the dead are warriors, and four of the wounded."

It was not as bad as Loomis had feared. He still had forty warrior monks among the effectives.

"Munitions?" he asked.

"We've used about two-thirds of the grenades, three-quarters of the rockets. Where we're really hurting is in ammo. We're down to about forty clips."

Loomis had expected that. But with the Uighur penchant for bandoliers, cartridges for the Mausers were plentiful. All salvation might lie in the captured weapons.

"Let's give the ammo to the ten best and retire the rest of the Kalashnikovs," he said. "Take all the warrior monks down to the barricade and teach them how to load and fire the Mausers. You can let them squeeze off a few rounds, get the feel of them."

"Right-oh," Owenby said. "And bye the bye, one of the Turks talked a bit before he died. He confirmed your guess that Oztrak himself is commanding out there. Didn't lead the charge, mind you, but directed from the rear like a true general."

Loomis thought of the handsome young man who had

led the charge. Apparently Oztrak picked his lieutenants well.

"The claymores did good work," Loomis said. "Can Drupa make more?"

Owenby shook his head. "No more bamboo. But Drupa asked me to remind you we still have those satchel charges you had him make. I think he's hurt you haven't used them."

"We will," Loomis promised. "I'm on my way to talk contingency plans with Lhalde and the lama. Tell the lookouts to keep a sharp eye on the Turks. If there's any movement, call me."

Owenby gave Loomis a quasi-military salute. He then shouted to the warrior monks and led the way toward the barricade. Loomis walked up the ridge and into the lamasery.

Lhalde and the Kamala Lama were waiting in a small prayer room off the main corridor. Loomis entered, closed the curtains behind him, and sank onto the proffered cushions. The lama regarded him solemnly.

"I congratulate you on a signal victory, Mr. Loomis. I'm told our warriors took a terrible toll on the enemy."

"We count two hundred and twenty-six," Loomis said. "Your warriors deserve the credit. They fought like seasoned veterans."

"Can we hold?" the lama asked.

"No," Loomis said. "Not through another assault like the last. Our ammunition for the Kalashnikovs is almost gone. We've lost the surprise of the rockets, the effectiveness of the monks. I can't put this into terms strong enough: we must prepare to abandon the lamasery."

Tears came to the lama's eyes. "How much time do we have to prepare?"

"That depends on the Turks," Loomis told him. "I expect them to attempt a flanking movement, over one ridge or the other. We should be able to prevent this, for the terrain is to our advantage. But they'll make another all-out charge tomorrow morning. It should be successful."

"Then we have less than twenty-four hours," Khalde said.

"Only if we're lucky," Loomis answered. "That timetable is guesswork. I could be wrong. Oztrak could attack this evening, before sundown."

"The *drokba* are three hours away," Lhalde said. "They need the darkness to conceal their movements. I'll send a runner to them now. What should I tell them?"

Loomis considered the question carefully. His estimate that the Uighurs would wait until the following day was only a hunch. But he felt he knew Oztrak's mind. He sensed that the man was thrown off stride by his heavy losses and a bit less sure of himself. He would need time to collect his wits, reorganize, plan the next full-scale attack. Until then there probably would be only probes, minor skirmishes.

Loomis made the decision, fully aware of the risks.

"Tell them we will evacuate tomorrow morning—at dawn."

"That will leave us little time to prepare," Lhalde said.

The Kamala Lama smiled. "But enough."

"There must be no delays," Loomis warned.

"We'll work all night," the lama promised. "We'll be ready."

"Then if you'll excuse me, I must make preparations of my own," Loomis said.

He returned to the entrenchments. Owenby came to him and pointed to the plain.

"The buggers are up to something. They've saddled their nags and formed up. But there seems to be something false about it. They're not whooping and yelling like this morning."

Loomis hurried down the ridge, with Owenby following. Lowering himself into the slit trench, Loomis raised his binoculars and studied the Uighur encampment.

The squadrons were in formation and maneuvering. But Owenby had good instincts. Something indeed seemed to be missing. The units did not show the same snap and polish as they had before the battle.

Yet the threat could not be ignored. The squadrons appeared to be preparing for a charge.

"Get the monks into position," Loomis ordered. "Pass the word for them to await my command before firing."

Owenby trotted away. Loomis continued to watch the Uighurs.

The squadrons practiced wheeling and marching around. Loomis could discern no purpose in it.

He glanced to the top of the mountain. The lookouts were signaling frantically. Loomis rose from the slit trench, stood on the parapet, and waved until he caught Owenby's attention. He pointed to the lookouts, then ran up the ridge to the barricade, where monks stood shading their eyes and voicing the signals aloud.

"Uighurs are climbing the north face of the left-hand ridge," Owenby translated.

Loomis winced. He should have guessed. The pony show out on the plains was a diversion, while the assault team attempted a flanking movement.

"How many?" he asked.

"They say about a hundred."

"Quick," Loomis told Owenby. "First-team grenadiers, first-team riflemen are to come with me. You and Khedru prepare for a frontal assault."

"What the hell will we do?" Owenby said.

"Same as this morning," Loomis said. "Hold your fire until they're right on top of you. Use the rest of the rockets if you have to. But save the satchel charges. I'll be back as soon as I can."

He led the twenty warrior monks out onto the left-hand ridge. Guided by the lookouts on top of the mountain, he moved until he was directly above the unseen Uighurs climbing up from below.

At this point the side of the ridge was less steep, dropping away at an angle of about forty-five degrees. Over this bare, rocky terrain wound a faint trail, apparently that used by the *drokba* bringing supplies up to the lamasery.

Loomis assigned each of the warriors to a position by

pointing. Once they were in position, the twenty riflemen formed a half circle around the exposed portion of the trail. Yet, by lying flat, the warriors could remain hidden from below.

With forefinger to lips Loomis warned the warriors to silence. He found a position for himself that commanded a view of both trail and the semicircle.

Then they waited.

A quarter of an hour passed before the first sounds came. Loomis first heard grunts, exclamations that might have been profanity, and the scraping of metal on rock. He hunkered lower behind the clumps of grass and rocks he was using for cover. Peeking through the grass, he could see the entire sweep of the trail below. He removed his .380 from its holster and held it against his cheek.

The Uighurs came up without much caution. Breathing hard from the altitude, they seemed oblivious to everything except the exertion of climbing. Overheated, they had unbuttoned their heavy sheepskin coats. Accustomed to life in the saddle, they carried their rifles carelessly, some using the butts as an alpenstock.

In the midst of the Uighurs, apparently their commander, was the handsome young man Loomis had seen earlier leading the charge.

Loomis held his breath, waiting, as more and more Uighurs came into view. They were moving painfully slowly. Each moment Loomis expected one of his warrior monks to yield to the strain and open fire. But the monks remained hidden, waiting. Loomis marveled over the discipline of his untrained troops. Arrayed along the switchbacks of the trail, more than fifty Uighurs were exposed along the slope.

When the leading Uighurs were within forty feet of the semicircle, Loomis brought up his pistol and opened fire. He shot three before reaction came from any quarter.

The monks fired their twenty rifles almost as one. The salvo felled almost half the Uighurs in sight. The rest withered under the sustained barrage. Only a few of the Uighurs in the rear managed to get off a single round.

Sporadic firing continued as the monks dispatched the wounded and exchanged shots with the Turks farther below.

Loomis rose to his feet and signaled for the monks to cease fire. More than forty Uighur dead lay motionless on the trail.

In the silence that followed Loomis heard shouting from down the trail. He selected three of the warrior monks and led them down through the dead Uighurs. The bodies lay crumpled, most shot through the heart or head.

At the point where the ridge dropped away, Loomis risked looking over the edge. He caught occasional glimpses of the Uighur survivors, retreating back down the side of the mountain.

One of the warrior monks made signs indicating he wished to follow and snipe-shoot the retreating Turks.

Loomis shook his head negatively. He felt he should get his twenty riflemen back to their defensive positions in case the cavalry made another full-scale attack.

Already the other monks were gathering rifles from among the dead and stripping the bodies of bandoliers.

Loomis led them back over the ridge to the lamasery entrance. There the fresh supply of rifles and ammunition was stacked beside the barricade. Loomis climbed up to the lamasery entrance for a better view of the cavalry, still arrayed out on the plain. Owenby came up to stand beside him.

"The buggers seem to be waiting for something," Owenby said. "They marched around awhile, even made a false charge or two. But for the last half hour they've just bloody well been sitting there."

"They're waiting for the signal that the flanking squadron is in place," Loomis said. "They won't get one."

"So what happens now?"

"We get ready for the attack tomorrow morning. I want you to drill every man on exactly what he is to do. I'll work with Drupa, lay the groundwork for the retreat."

"The men want to dig in and try to hold them," Owenby reported. "They say we did it the first time."

In his better moments Loomis was tempted to agree. But he remembered the fury of the Uighur charge. This time there would be no surprise, such as the rockets, the sustained, deadly fire from the Kalashnikovs.

"No," Loomis said. "This time Oztrak will throw in his reserves. We won't have the firepower to hold them."

"The men feel that retreat is an even bigger risk."

"Maybe," Loomis conceded. "But not if we do it right."

Owenby was silent for a time. When he again spoke, his voice was unnatural, filled with emotion.

"Loomis, old sod, don't shit me. Do we have any chance at all of getting out of this alive?"

Loomis had been wondering the same thing.

"It depends on timing," he said. "Timing will be everything."

At sunset the muezzin sounded the cry for worship. Oztrak left his tent and joined his men in prayer.

With the low rays of the sun silhouetting the mountain range and hundreds of voices raised in appeals to Allah, the ceremony was impressive. The sounds echoed off the mountainside, so Oztrak was certain his enemies also were listening.

Yet he could not contain his fury sufficiently to concentrate on his prayers. He felt he could not be blamed for the failure of the initial charge. No one would have anticipated the clever defense executed by the warrior monks. But now with the failure of the flanking movement, Oztrak felt culpable. Even worse, he sensed that the men were beginning to question his leadership. Tomorrow he must prove himself.

On rising from his devotions, Oztrak returned to his tent. Erek still lay on a sheepskin robe. His wound had been tended, but clearly he had not yet recovered from his ordeal.

"They were waiting, my commander," Erek said. "I

was careless. I should have had men walking point. We stumbled into it blindly."

Oztrak sat down beside him. True, Erek had been careless. No doubt Pishan had been careless. Gungor, camping on the plain, had not bothered to post guards.

"From the beginning, we have underestimated the American," Oztrak said. "Tomorrow will be different. Our attack will utilize every man to the fullest. And we'll spring a few surprises of our own."

"We will succeed. I know it," Erek said. "I won't stop until I reach the lamasery entrance."

Oztrak looked at Erek's leg. His leather trousers had been cut away and the bullet wound bandaged.

"You're not well enough," Oztrak said. "I'll let Batu command the charge."

"Maybe I can't walk," Erek said. "But I can ride. I'm going, my commander. I wouldn't miss it for the world."

13

The first bugles sounded on the plain well before sunup. Loomis left his work with the explosives, went to the end of the right-hand ridge, and watched as Oztrak organized his forces. Soon Loomis could see a pattern.

More squadrons were being brought up front, to form a wide-angle wedge.

The formation would yield a much greater concentration of firepower, and Loomis had no effective resources for meeting it. As he had anticipated, Oztrak was not holding any squadrons in reserve. All were arrayed in the new formation.

Loomis monitored the Uighurs until, at sunup, he heard the muezzin cry out the call to worship. The Uighurs dismounted, unrolled their prayer rugs, and knelt facing Mecca.

Knowing the ceremony would keep them occupied at least a half hour, Loomis hurried back up the ridge to the entrenchments below the entrance to the lamasery. There he called Owenby, Lhalde, Khedru, and Drupa into a hurried conference.

"Are you ready?" he asked Lhalde.

"Almost," Lhalde said. "The work has gone on all night. Everyone is tired. But we'll be ready in about another four hours."

"Too long," Loomis said. "Oztrak will begin his attack in about forty-five minutes. We'll be lucky if we hold him off an hour. That gives you less than two hours. You must be prepared to abandon the lamasery by then."

Lhalde's brow wrinkled in renewed worry. "Much yet remains to be done. The manuscripts must be wrapped carefully for protection. That takes time. It can't be rushed."

"It'll have to be," Loomis said. "In two hours Oztrak's army will probably be inside. You've got to have all your men out."

Lhalde's hesitation was brief. "I'll see what I can do to speed matters."

Owenby was translating for Khedru and Drupa.

"Ask Drupa if all charges are in place," Loomis said. After a brief exchange, Owenby had the answer.

"He says they're installed precisely where you ordered. The detonators are with each charge, but not yet attached, as you instructed."

"Good," Loomis said. Maybe one facet of the plan was being done right.

"What about our warrior monks?" Loomis asked Owenby. "Are you sure they know exactly what's expected of them?"

"I've told them, over and over. They know what they're to do. But whether they'll remember in the heat of battle, I haven't the foggiest."

"You can rest assured they'll follow orders," Lhalde said. "They've been doing so all their adult lives."

"I hope they remember that today," Loomis said. "Owenby, tell Khedru to impress this upon them. We can't have any false heroics screwing up the works."

"Right-oh," Owenby said.

"And you watch for my signals. We must act in unison. There can be no slipups."

"It'll go like clockwork," Owenby said.

"And, Lhalde, when the time comes, we'll proceed with the plan, assuming you and your men are out of the way."

Lhalde nodded.

"Okay, good luck," Loomis said.

He walked back down the ridge to the forward slit trenches. The warrior monks lay in their holes, calmly awaiting the assault. A few were working their prayer wheels, but most seemed to be meditating. Across the way, on the opposite ridge, Owenby was talking as he walked past his men.

Loomis wished he had enough command of the Tibetan language to do the same. He still harbored doubts that the warrior monks could carry out his elaborate plan.

Oztrak's cavalry was back in the saddle, apparently awaiting the signal to attack. Loomis studied the formations carefully. He surmised that Oztrak still had more than seven hundred fighting men to hurl against the surviving forty warrior monks.

Slowly the minutes dragged by. Loomis assumed Oztrak was awaiting the proper moment, when the bright rays of the early morning sun would be directly at his back, low on the horizon.

The day was perfect, the air clear and crisp, with only a hint of high cirrus clouds against the blue sky. In such perfection it was difficult to believe that within the next two hours hundreds of men would die.

But that was always the way. No day ever seemed appropriate for death.

Again bugles sounded on the plain. Abruptly the Uighurs shifted into an even tighter formation, with the forwardmost elements moving together, melding into a tightly knit prong. Behind them, other squadrons moved up. Within seconds, the mass of cavalry turned itself into a compact wedge.

Loomis understood the purpose of the maneuver. With the tightly packed angle, more guns could be brought to bear on the ridges. The forward prong, riding down the middle of the plain, would remain out of range of the grenadiers.

Upon more bugle calls, the Uighurs began to move. Loomis picked up a Kalashnikov. Ammunition for the weapon was almost completely exhausted, but enough remained that he had positioned four of the automatics at strategic points. He himself had only three clips left.

On further bugle commands, the Uighurs moved into a trot, then a gallop. The steady drumming of the horses' hooves rolled up the valley like thunder. Loomis glanced behind him. All of his men were in place.

The leading squadron came down the middle of the valley, as he expected. A few shots were wasted as some of the monks opened fire too early. But the remaining grenadiers were not lured into throwing their grenades beyond their range. The point squadron swept on past, charging full-tilt for the barricade directly below the lamasery entrance, riding over the bodies of their comrades killed in the battle only twenty-four hours before.

At the barricade they met a withering barrage from the warrior monks. Almost simultaneously, the flying wedge came within range of the ridges, and the remainder of the warrior monks opened fire. The grenadiers hurled grenades into the tightly packed mass.

For a moment the attack faltered. All forward momentum was lost.

Then the bulk of the reserves swept into the valley, carrying the other squadrons before it. The Uighurs milled along each ridge, pouring bullets into the defenders. Their own grenadiers attacked, riding out of the center of the formations, swinging bowling-ball-sized grenades in nets. They hurled them onto the top of the ridges, where they exploded with awesome roars.

Loomis fired into the throng, knocking riders from their horses. But the mass of Uighurs moved steadily, relentlessly up the valley toward the lamasery entrance.

Although the Tibetans were taking a terrible toll, Loomis knew they could not hold. It was time.

He rose out of the slit trench and raised an arm. Across

the way, Owenby saw his signal and answered with his own.

Loomis turned and gave the word. The closest warrior monk left his hole and began the retreat.

Loomis glanced across the valley. Already Owenby's first man was running along the ridge.

In relay fashion, a man at a time, the monks were in retreat along both ridges. Loomis was folding up his defense like an accordion, concentrating his forces at the barricade in front of the lamasery entrance.

Confident that all was going well, Loomis resumed shooting. He was down to his last clip. He shifted to single fire, burning a round only on the most certain targets.

Soon his rifle was empty and he was alone on the ridge. All the monks had retreated. Across the way, Owenby was just leaving his position. So far, the retreat was working well.

Loomis smashed his now-useless Kalashnikov on a rock and abandoned the trench. He ran along the ridge toward the entrenchment. On the way he passed the bodies of two warrior monks. He paused to pick up a Mauser and two bandoliers of ammunition.

The Uighurs were now circling in orderly fashion in front of the central barrier, a maneuver that not only turned them into moving, uncertain targets, but also gave each rider ample time to work the bolt of his rifle and locate a new target.

Occasionally the Uighur grenadiers broke through the circling riders and hurled their bombs over the barricade. Each explosion sprayed deadly shrapnel over a wide area.

The last of the retreating monks leaped into the horseshoe-shaped entrenchment below the lamasery entrance. Loomis brought up the rear of the retreat, making certain each trench was empty. He passed the bodies of three more warrior monks. Pausing to be sure they were dead, he collected their ammunition and took it with him.

With the concentrated defense at the barricade, the battle there intensified. Adhering to the techniques Loomis had taught them, the Tibetans worked in two-man teams, one up firing, the other clearing a spent round and chambering another.

Steadily the number of dead and wounded in front of the barricade mounted. Yet the Uighurs kept pressing, riding right up to the breastworks to fire their weapons.

Loomis caught a glimpse of the handsome young officer he had seen in the two previous battles. Impeccably dressed in a military-styled tunic, with flowing black beard and moustache, waving a sword to urge his men forward, the young man looked like something out of a history book.

Loomis put him in his sights and squeezed off a round. But at that moment the man's horse wheeled. The bullet apparently missed by inches. Loomis tried once more, and again the horse turned at the wrong moment.

The young officer seemed to be enjoying a charmed life. He disappeared into the melee.

Owenby came to Loomis out of the smoke, dust, and confusion.

"We can't hold on the left, old sod," he shouted. "We'd best get the hell out of here."

"Not yet," Loomis yelled back. "We'll wait for the big one."

Less than five minutes later it came. The Uighurs drew back two hundred meters and gathered into a massive formation. With the handsome young officer leading, they came in an all-out charge at the barricade, intending to overwhelm the monks by sheer numbers.

Loomis moved forward, dropped into prone position, and took careful aim. He waited until the charging Uighurs were on top of the explosives before he fired. His bullet struck the detonator—a bundle of fulminate-of-mercury caps.

The whole world seemed to explode. Even though Loomis had supervised the placing of the charges, he was surprised by the awesome results of the blast. Horses and men were hurled skyward. For meters in every direction horses and men were knocked flat.

All firing ceased. Stunned, the surviving Uighurs drew back.

Rising from their trenches, the monks fled toward the entrance to the lamasery. Loomis lingered only long enough to make certain no wounded were left behind, then he also ran into the lamasery.

Owenby came to him exhilarated. "Worked like a bloody charm! We stopped the bastards cold!"

"Just for the moment," Loomis said. "Find Khedru. Tell him to go get Lhalde started. Tell him to stay with the monks and to keep them moving, no matter what. Tell him we'll not be far behind and that we'll catch up with him in a day or two."

"We don't have enough men left for the fallback," Owenby said. "Want me to take some from Khedru?"

"How many did you lose?"

"Six."

Loomis added his five. Eleven from forty left only twenty-nine warrior monks, and Khedru had fifteen of them.

"No, Khedru may need them. We have enough to do the job."

A moment later Khedru and his men hurried on down the main corridor. Loomis, Owenby, and the remaining monks darkened the lamps, took up positions, and waited.

Oztrak's troops were slow to recover from the blast. But after several minutes a group cautiously approached the lamasery entrance. Loomis allowed them to enter before opening fire. His men put down a barrage that sent the Uighurs back out of the cave in full retreat, leaving eight dead behind them.

"Maybe we should have made our stand here," Owenby said. "That was easy."

"Won't be next time," Loomis predicted.

The Uighurs began shooting into the corridor blindly with at least fifty rifles, apparently intending for the volume of lead to clear the way. Bullets riccocheted off the stone walls and whined down the corridor into the darkness. Loomis and his men took cover, not revealing their positions with return fire. The barrage lasted several minutes.

"They've probably sent back to camp for some bloody torches," Owenby said. "It never occurred to the sods it'd be dark in here."

At last the firing ceased as the Uighurs waited for the torches. Then again the Uighurs entered the cave, making good use of cover, dodging from place to place, crawling when necessary.

The first torch bearer was easily shot. But then the Uighurs began tossing torches ahead of them. Each of the torches, burning on the bare stone floor, lit a long length of corridor.

"Shit," Owenby said. "They've outfoxed us with that wrinkle."

Even as he ducked behind a ledge and lit the fuse that would seal the lamasery, Loomis wondered how badly his schedule would be affected by the Uighurs' unexpected maneuver with the torches.

From this point, every second was essential. Yet they could not make a stand in the glare of the torches.

"Let's fall back," he said.

Owenby passed the word. They ran down the corridor to the next position and waited in darkness. But the Uighurs did not hesitate. They came on, hurling the blazing torches well ahead, using the light as a shield.

Loomis and his men each fired a clip into the darkness beyond the torches.

Then on his order they again retreated.

Loomis checked the luminous dial on his watch. All was happening much too fast, and he could think of no immediate way to delay the Uighurs. By now hundreds of them must be in the corridors, exploring, taking possession.

He remembered the Kamala Lama's vision of the enemy filling the lamasery. It was happening.

Loomis began holding each position as long as possible, gradually regaining valuable minutes on his schedule. The corridor leading from the entrance to the air vent was just under a half mile in length. Halting for a stand every forty or fifty yards, Loomis and his men kept retreating.

At last they reached the narrow air shaft.

"Everybody out," Loomis ordered through Owenby. "Get the fire started."

He lingered to empty a clip into the darkness while Owenby and the monks scrambled down the air shaft. Then he quickly followed.

He climbed out of the bell-shaped terminal of the air shaft into the open air. Lhalde, Khedru, and the monks were already far out on the plain, the treasures from their lamasery loaded onto a long caravan of yaks and sheep tended by the loyal *drokba.* With any luck, the intervening ridges would keep them hidden from the Uighur encampment until they had put considerable distance behind them.

"Light the fire," Loomis ordered through Owenby. "We don't have much time."

In bringing the yaks and sheep up to the air shaft for loading, the *drokba* had brought along an ample supply of both dried and green grass. The warrior monks lit the pile of dry grass beside the air intake. Flames instantly soared over the huge mound. As the monks dumped green grass on the blaze, dense smoke poured into the lamasery, along with air partially depleted of oxygen.

Fortunately the prevailing wind had held, sucking all the smoke into the lamasery.

"How many buggers you think are in there?" Owenby asked.

Loomis had been trying to estimate. From the drumming of footsteps on the stone floor of the corridor, he felt they had drawn most of Oztrak's force into the lamasery.

"Two or three hundred at least," he said. "Maybe more."

"Shitty way to go," Owenby said. "Couldn't happen to nicer people."

Loomis thought of the hundreds of men choking in that confined space, trying to make their way back down the corridors to the entrance in darkness.

He glanced at his watch. Due to the miscalculation in timing, some might make it. If he had misjudged what Oztrak would do next, all might be lost.

"Tell them to get those animals up here," Loomis said. "We'll leave as soon as it blows."

"How long?" Owenby asked.

"Six minutes."

Smoke continued to pour into the lamasery. Owenby sent two of the monks for the yaks, secreted in a hollow a hundred yards below the air intake.

Impatiently, Loomis waited as his watch counted off the minutes.

But apparently Drupa had misjudged the burning time for the fuse. The explosives went off almost two minutes early. The muffled roar of the blast came up the length of the corridor, sending a huge puff of smoke back out of the intake.

The force of the explosion was impressive. Loomis assumed it had done its work and that the entrance to the lamasery was sealed by tons of rock and dirt from the collapsed ceiling.

"Okay, let's close this one," Loomis said. "Everyone get moving. This is a short fuse."

Owenby and the monks mounted their yaks and moved away. Loomis waited until they were in the clear. He then lit the fuse and ran after them.

Owenby was holding a yak for Loomis. Jumping into the saddle, he managed to make another thirty yards before the charge exploded. Even so, fist-sized chunks of rock were hurled past them by the blast.

Loomis looked back. The overhang had dropped. The

air intake was closed. Hundreds of Oztrak's Uighurs were sealed in the smoke-filled lamasery.

Loomis and his men rode toward the southwest, hurrying after Lhalde and his caravan. Loomis kept looking back, watching for movement on the plain.

He had no doubt that Oztrak would soon be in pursuit. The question was when.

14

The moment smoke poured out of the lamasery entrance Oztrak ordered recall sounded, for he knew instantly that he had sent his men into a trap. But even as the bugle blared he recognized that it was a useless gesture. Most of his men were too far into the lamasery to hear the bugle. He also realized belatedly that they would be shouting and staggering about in the dark, choking on the acrid fumes, trying to make their way back to the entrance.

He now knew he had erred badly in accepting the imbecile's word that only one entrance existed. He should have foreseen that the imbecile might not have been acquainted with other outlets to the lamasery, since the front entrance was the only one in everyday use. He should have listened to Batu and searched the mountain for other air vents. Now his lack of perception was costing him a goodly portion of his command.

He hurried forward to the entrance, but there he hesitated in indecision, reluctant to send more men inside in a rescue effort. The rescuers would be no more immune to the smoke than the victims. Most likely a premature rescue effort would only sacrifice the lives of more of his troops. He also was concerned that this might be only the opening phase of another of Loomis's tricks.

So he stood in uncharacteristic inaction and waited until the first of his men stumbled out of the entrance choking, blinded by smoke.

The sad spectacle of their helplessness at last spurred Oztrak to life. He promptly ordered the choking victims taken away from the entrance, to purer air out on the plain. He observed with disgust that in their panic most of the men had thrown away their arms.

Standing just outside the entrance, Oztrak suddenly was knocked flat by a tremendous explosion. Stunned, lying full length on the ground, he looked up to see clouds of dust, not smoke, boiling out of the lamasery.

The dust and lack of smoke told him that the shaft was sealed, with hundreds of his men inside, suffocating.

Temporarily deafened, badly shaken, Oztrak staggered to his feet. Blood ran freely from his nose. Around him, his aides began to stir.

Oztrak's first thought was of Erek, who had led the charge into the lamasery. By now he would be far inside, trapped.

As Oztrak stood wondering about the feasibility of attempting to find the air intake that had pushed the smoke through the lamasery, the dull boom of a second explosion came from the other side of the mountain. Oztrak felt certain the explosion meant that the second outlet also was sealed. If so, Erek and fully a third of the *jihad* army were buried—possibly still alive—somewhere inside the mountain.

Ignoring outstretched hands attempting to help him, Oztrak fought his way through the dust and debris until he was inside the entrance to the lamasery.

A torch lay on the floor of the corridor. Oztrak picked it up. An aide helped him light it. Holding it high, Oztrak walked on into the corridor.

For twenty yards into the lamasery the vaulted ceiling remained intact. Only at the point of the explosion had the roof collapsed, allowing a portion of the mountain to fall into the corridor, blocking it.

Oztrak came to grips with a crucial decision: Loomis and Lhalde no doubt had left the lamasery by the air shaft and were now fleeing to safety. He should be in pursuit. Out in the open, Loomis's tricks would not help him. Strung out in a caravan, with many noncombatants to defend, he would be at a disadvantage. Even with reduced numbers, Oztrak easily could destroy Loomis's much smaller force.

But immediate pursuit would require abandonment of Erek and perhaps three hundred men sealed in the mountain, possibly still alive.

Oztrak raised his torch and studied the vaulted ceiling. Only a meter away from the cave-in the heavy overhead stones remained intact, firmly in place, without even a crack between them. Clearly the ceiling was basically strong. Chances were good that the vaulted arch also held on the other side of the blast area.

Quite possibly only three or four meters of the overhead arch had collapsed. He might be able to dig through in time to save Erek and the three hundred men still in the shaft. He also needed to recover the weapons his men had dropped in their panic, for he now had more men than rifles. He also might need the ammunition Erek and his men were carrying.

There were other considerations. If he abandoned Erek and the men, the remainder of his command would never forgive, nor forget. Morale would plummet. Also, he needed time for the men to recover from the shock. If the loss of life was as high as he anticipated, he would need to reorganize his command.

Yet, even with the delay, he still would be able to catch up with Loomis in a matter of days. His horses were twice as fast as Loomis's yaks. Traveling with three hundred fifty monks and no doubt hundreds of animals, Loomis would be leaving a plain trail. Oztrak would have no difficulty following him.

After considering the matter, Oztrak felt confident he

had sufficient time to attempt a rescue, to recover the weapons, to reorganize, and to catch up with Loomis.

"Quick!" he shouted. "Everyone! Start digging!"

He put every able-bodied man to work. But without proper equipment, progress was excruciatingly slow. Before long the rescue effort fell into a routine. Oztrak ordered a fire built, both for warmth and for light in the corridor.

As darkness fell his men became more adept. They brought horses up to the entrance and strapped on them crude baskets made from saddle leather and sheepskin. Wielding leather scoops, the men shoveled the dirt into the baskets to be taken away from the site and dumped.

Gradually the pile of dirt and rock in the corridor diminished. With plain evidence of their progress, the men renewed their efforts.

For a time Oztrak worried that more of the mountain might come down, wiping out all they had accomplished. But by keeping the tunneling effort small, and by shoring up constantly with rocks, they managed to keep fresh cave-ins to a minimum.

The men labored throughout the night. Shortly after dawn, the diggers broke through into the inner shaft. Oztrak called for two volunteers. With lines attached to their waists, two young Uighurs crawled through, carrying torches.

Within seconds both men collapsed and their torches sputtered out. Hurriedly the line handlers dragged them back to safety. In this way Oztrak learned that the air inside was poisonous and that Erek and his men were dead.

Still, he needed the weapons and ammunition. He sent teams to explore the mountain, seeking other air shafts.

At midmorning the site of the distant explosion was found. When word came, Oztrak ordered his horse and rode around the mountain and made his way up to it.

He found only disappointment. The blast had topped an overhanging ledge of rock, apparently sealing the air vent. After examining the site, Oztrak decided that the amount of digging required to reopen the shaft was beyond his immediate capabilities.

Shortly afterward, a second, smaller air shaft was found, high up on the side of the mountain. Apparently it was used only for venting heat and fumes from the kitchens. But it soon proved amazingly efficient. Within minutes after the louvered control arrangement was removed, stale air moved at gale force through the crawl hole at the entrance, expelling the poisonous air from the interior.

After an hour of ventilation, Oztrak risked sending two more men into the lamasery. They remained on their feet and their torches continued to burn brightly.

Oztrak crawled through the hole into the lamasery. As he expected, the ceiling in the interior remained intact.

He walked deeper into the lamasery with his men. Beyond the first turn, bodies lay everywhere. Most apparently had died of suffocation, although caked blood indicated that some had been trampled in panic.

Not one man was found alive.

Erek's body lay at the end of the main corridor, where it narrowed into the air shaft. Oztrak assumed that Erek had been among the first to fall when the corridors filled with smoke.

Even in death, Erek was strikingly handsome with his full beard, finely chiseled features, and black moustache. Standing over him, Oztrak could not hold back tears.

He ordered the remainder of the lamasery searched thoroughly, but no valuables were found—not even so much as a rug or wall hanging. Apparently Lhalde had taken all the lamasery furnishings with him.

"Collect the weapons and ammunition," Oztrak ordered.

Briefly he considered removing the bodies for burial outside the lamasery. But he felt he did not have the time to waste. Already Loomis was a full day ahead of him.

After ordering his men out of the lamasery, he directed the placement of explosives for some length along the ceiling near the entrance.

When all was ready, he lit the fuse himself. The resulting explosion brought down more of the mountain, closing not only the small tunnel his men had dug, but also the main corridor for many meters. No doubt Erek, his men, and the lamasery would remain buried forever.

That evening Oztrak drafted a new organizational chart for his vastly reduced command. He was aware that most of the men assumed the mission had failed and that with morning they would be turning back toward home. But Oztrak felt differently.

Counting Pishan in the pass, Gungor on the plain, and the battles around the lamasery, Loomis now had destroyed more than six hundred of his men—almost two-thirds of the entire *jihad* army. Even by scraping the bottom of the barrel with untrained reserves, Oztrak would be able to field only three hundred and fifty men.

Even worse, his best commanders were gone—Pishan and Gungor, Erek and Batu. Oztrak badly missed Pishan and Gungor. And he grieved for Erek. He was beyond anger; revenge had become an obsession. He had no choice but to go after Loomis.

How could he return to Turpan with a third of his army and no victory? Only a resounding success in the field could wipe out his shame. When he returned to Turpan, he must be bearing the severed heads of Loomis, Lhalde, and the Kamala Lama. Nothing less would do.

He contemplated his chart of reorganization through much of the night. With an abundance of arms and horses, he felt he must put them to maximum use. But he lacked a single experienced commander he could trust.

He considered his choices carefully. Toward dawn he sent for Kiyak, a young assistant squadron commander who had shown promise. He reported promptly to Oztrak's tent and stood expectant, ramrod straight. Studying him, Oztrak felt reassured that he had made a good choice.

True, Kiyak was young—no more than nineteen—but he was intelligent and conscientious. He lacked experience. The charges against the lamasery had been his introduction to battle. But in training he stood out sufficiently that his promotions had come rapidly. He had dark, alert eyes, a full beard and moustache, and a tall, muscular body. He spoke in a rich, melodious baritone.

"I am reporting as ordered, my commander. I am at your service."

"I've selected you to replace Erek as my second-in-command," Oztrak told him. "You may pick your own replacement to command your squadron."

Kiyak could not conceal his amazement and pleasure. He stood even taller, his eyes sparkling.

"I am honored, my commander. I gladly will give my life to fulfill the trust you have placed in me."

Oztrak waved a hand impatiently. "We've much work to do. I've made a revised chart of organization, a new chain of command. Memorize it. At first light, we'll form new squadrons out of the old. An hour later, the squadrons must be prepared to march."

"I hear you, my commander. It will be done."

Kiyak hurried off to memorize the new chart. Oztrak pulled out his map of the western high plateau and sat studying it, wondering where Loomis and Lhalde were headed.

He was eager to set out in pursuit. But he felt that his men first needed some sense of accomplishment. He devised a plan to give them this, along with a taste of blood to inspire them.

In his witless way, the imbecile had confirmed that the lamasery long had been kept supplied with food by the native *drokba*. Now Loomis and Lhalde were fleeing with the lamasery, carried by yaks and sheep no doubt supplied by these same loyal Buddhist *drokba*.

Oztrak and his command were sworn to stamp out Buddhism—and Buddhists—wherever found. He had received permission from the Red Chinese to do so. Several hundred Buddhist *drokba* had been living near the mountain, supplying Lhalde and the Kamala Lama food and essentials. Oztrak intended to make their destruction his first order of business.

At dawn he summoned his shrunken army into its new formation. It now consisted of three squadrons of cavalry plus a reduced headquarters corps.

After naming the new squadron commanders, Oztrak faced his troops and raised his voice so all could hear.

"The enemies of Allah are clever," he said. "They have cost us dearly. We now must show that we are truly courageous, worthy of the task assigned us."

He paused and rode along the ranks of his men, looking into their eyes.

"We have two courses open to us," he shouted. "We can go home and spend our lives grieving for our comrades. Or we can go after the enemy and see to it that our comrades have not fallen in vain."

From somewhere in the rear ranks a strong voice called out: *"Jihad!"* Instantly the cry was taken up by three hundred fifty voices. The word rose to the skies and bounced back from the mountain: *"Jihad! Jihad! Jihad!"*

Oztrak allowed the momentum of the chant to build. Then he raised a hand for silence.

"I see I do not need to remind all of you that you have pledged your lives to the *jihad.* I promise you that today you will be called upon to demonstrate your devotion to the *jihad,* to the glory of Allah."

Within the hour they broke camp and set out around the small range of mountains. Oztrak rode in the lead with Kiyak. In midafternoon they came upon the abandoned site of a *drokba* encampment.

All signs indicated that the camp had long been in use. Oztrak was aware that although the word *drokba* meant nomad, and that these *drokba* thought of themselves as such, in actual practice they often maintained a permanent home camp for years, while driving their animals to distant pastures for varying periods.

Plainly this had been such a home base. Yet it had been abandoned overnight, simultaneously with the departure of the lamasery. Oztrak had no doubt that these were some of the *drokba* who had kept the lamasery supplied and who had helped Loomis and Lhalde in making their escape.

He led his army along the plain trail left by the *drokba*. It crossed the flat grasslands to the west, and Oztrak observed that the nomads did not pause to graze their animals, as they would do ordinarily. Clearly they were fleeing the site of the lamasery.

In late afternoon Oztrak and his army came upon the new *drokba* camp beside a small lake. On sighting the Uighurs, the natives fled on foot in every direction.

Oztrak spoke to Kiyak. "Kill them. Kill them all."

"I hear you, my commander," Kiyak said. "It will be done."

Oztrak sat on his horse beside the lake and watched his squadrons sweep down on the fleeing nomads. Some were shot, others were dispatched with rifle butts. A few were beheaded with swords and others disemboweled with long knives.

Within a quarter of an hour the slaughter was completed. Seventy-three Tibetan Buddhists—men, women, and children—lay dead around the small lake.

Oztrak rode among them on an inspection tour. He was pleased with the results. The destruction of the entire encampment had been efficiently done.

"Search the tents," he ordered.

The camp yielded a wealth of badly needed supplies—cheeses, yogurt, cured mutton, roasted barley. Apparently the *drokba* had prepared for the coming winter with a huge harvest of hay. Oztrak ordered it bailed and loaded on the spare horses along with the rest of the supplies.

The looted supplies lifted his spirits. Despite his recent setbacks, all was not lost.

In many ways he now was better prepared for a long pursuit than when he left Turpan. His command was leaner and required less upkeep. With fewer riders, but the same number of horses, he now possessed an abun-dance of pack animals. He could keep them loaded with the gleanings from his victories. He intended to make a sweep through the whole region, clearing it of Buddhist natives.

But first he would pursue and deal with Loomis.

At sundown, after evening prayers, they feasted beside the lake, on the site of their victory. In the twilight Oztrak's men entertained themselves with a game of rugby, played with a severed head. Mildly amused, Oztrak watched the sport for a time. He then returned to his tent and retired early.

On the following morning, hardly more than two hours after sunup, Oztrak struck the trail of Loomis and Lhalde. To his surprise, it led west-southwest. He had assumed that Loomis would be traveling southeast, fleeing toward the border of Nepal.

What could be Loomis's destination? Oztrak looked at his map. He could not imagine. He wondered if the lamasery had another hideout somewhere along the disputed borders of Tibet, Pakistan, Afghanistan, and India, in the region of Jammu and Kashmir.

Oztrak summoned Kiyak.

"Attend me well," he said. "We'll maintain a forced march from this moment until the enemy is sighted. We'll stop only for the obligatory morning and evening prayers. The trail left by the enemy is plain. We'll follow it by moonlight, even by starlight if necessary. Tell the men they will eat and piss in the saddle in the fashion of their ancestors. And you may convey to them my promise that at the end of this long, hard ride, they will enjoy a victory."

"I hear you, my commander," Kiyak said. "It shall be done."

As Kiyak galloped back to give the order to his squadron commanders, Oztrak observed how well he sat in the saddle, so proud and erect, so handsome and manly. There was something about him that reminded Oztrak of Erek. Perhaps even of his dead oldest son.

15

We're moving too slowly," Loomis said. "We must do better. I can't understand why Oztrak hasn't caught up with us by now."

"Maybe the sod has given up," Owenby said. "Maybe we bloodied his nose even worse than we thought."

"Oztrak hasn't given up," the Kamala Lama said quietly. "He'll keep after us as long as he is left with a single man."

Owenby translated the discussion for Khedru, who shook his head in disagreement.

"To the contrary, our animals must have more time to rest," Khedru replied through Owenby. "If we continue at this pace, they soon will begin to deteriorate."

"I fear he's right, Mr. Loomis," Lhalde said. "And we need the animals. We can't hope to survive in this desolate country without them. Especially in this storm."

They were seated around a dung fire—Loomis, Owenby, Lhalde, Khedru, and the lama. All day they had fled westward, driving the animals to the limit of endurance, constantly maintaining a rear guard against pursuit.

The storm had struck out of the northwest before noon, bringing ice, snow, high winds, and temperatures well below zero Farenheit. As Lhalde had observed, the long, mild fall apparently had ended and they were experiencing the first storm of the oncoming Himalayan winter.

With darkness they had camped in a shallow ravine, one of few to be found on the flat landscape. They had no tents. Lean-to shelters were their only protection against the icy wind.

Lhalde and the Kamala Lama, unaccustomed to exposure to the elements, were shivering beside the flickering fire even though they were thoroughly wrapped in quilted blankets. On the fringes of the camp a few of the monks were feeding the yaks and sheep. Others were cooking supper.

Loomis was pleased that discipline had not broken down during the arduous forced march. The monks not only performed their duties of the trail, but also managed to continue their religious obligations, chanting their mantras and working their prayer wheels on the move.

Tonight there would be no moon. A strong wind was still blowing out of the northwest. The air was growing even colder.

Loomis was worried. With his awkward caravan of hundreds of yaks and sheep, he could not hope to outrun Oztrak's horses.

He knew Khedru was right. He had been setting a killing pace for the animals. And as Lhalde had observed, the animals were their only means of survival in this barren land.

Lhalde had done an amazing job of organization in the evacuation of the lamasery. More than two hundred yaks and a hundred sheep had been brought from the *drokba* camp to the air intake on the side of the mountain. There the animals had been loaded—each yak allotted two hundred pounds of cargo and each sheep sixty. Loading had continued right up to the last stages of the battle at the entrance.

Loomis could not dismiss the horrors he had committed. He had always been bothered afterward by battle deaths—of his comrades, of the men he himself had killed. But he found some comfort in the knowledge that no other course had existed. He knew that if he had not utilized the plan, the Uighurs would have slain all the monks and destroyed one of mankind's most valuable legacies—the manuscripts. Yet he could not shake the terrible visions of what he had done.

Now, only three days later, they were more than a hundred miles west of the lamasery. Throughout those three days, Loomis had kept hand-picked men a few miles back, watching for pursuit. Thus far, none had been sighted. Yet pursuit was inevitable. And he was growing increasingly convinced that he could not outrun Oztrak.

In his spare moments he had been studying maps of the western section of Tibet. He saw only one hope.

"Tomorrow we'll turn more to the northwest," he announced.

Owenby shoved his protective face mask aside. "Are you daft? That'd take us *away* from the passes into India. That's poor country up there. No water, less grass."

"But it's high," Loomis pointed out. "According to the map, that part of the high plateau is nearly eighteen thousand feet. My only question is for Khedru. Can our animals work and survive at that altitude?"

Owenby put the question to Khedru in Tibetan. Khedru apparently understood Loomis's tactics immediately. He smiled as he gave Owenby a long reply.

"He says if our yaks and sheep are allowed time to rest and to graze, they won't suffer at that altitude. He says you also might wish to consider that grazing would make our grain last longer."

Loomis nodded his understanding. Many of the sheep were carrying grain and hay both for themselves and for the yaks. From his own boyhood days on a ranch in Texas, Loomis knew that working animals needed supplementary grain. Khedru was saying that with sufficient grazing on the last of the summer grass and with the benefit of a slower pace, the grain rations could be cut.

"Then we'll turn to the northwest, and the high country," Loomis said.

"That's insane!" Owenby protested. "Right now we're only a bit more than two hundred miles from the passes into India. We could make a dash for it and be home safe."

Loomis had considered such a dash from every angle.

"We'd never make it," he said. "We're still outnumbered at least ten to one. Out here in the open, Oztrak has all the advantage. He could hang back and attack us time after time, chew us up by degrees."

"But why turn the wrong way? You think he won't follow us there?"

"I'm hoping it'll even the odds. Think about it. Oztrak and his men—and their horses—are from the Turpan Sink, one of the lowest spots on the face of the earth. Surely they lack the oxygen-carrying hemogoblin you talk about. At high altitude his horses may fail him. Ask Khedru about it."

Owenby explained Loomis's plan in Tibetan. Khedru answered at length. Owenby translated the reply.

"He says the altitude won't hurt our animals, as long as we don't overdo it. But he's fairly sure that if Oztrak pushes his horses, he'll kill them. He says they probably could only walk short distances at that altitude before stopping to fill their lungs with air."

The Kamala Lama had been listening silently to the exchange. He rearranged his blanket to free his mouth to speak.

"What route are you considering?" he asked Loomis.

Loomis brought out a map and spread it in the light of the fire, holding it flat on his knee against the wind. He traced the route with a forefinger.

"We'll go generally west by northwest until about here. Then we'll turn south again, along this high ridge, and follow it to where it joins the steppes of the Himalayas."

"That's six or seven hundred miles," Owenby said.

"Add two or three hundred over the passes into India. You're talking about a bloody thousand miles! In winter!"

Loomis ignored him. He pointed to the map. "Once we reach about here, on the approaches to the Himalayas, the ground appears more broken," he explained to the Kamala Lama. "From all indications on the map, I believe we may find good places to fight delaying actions. The altitude and terrain will be in our favor."

"But not the distance," Owenby insisted. "Our supplies won't last. We'd never make it."

"As the sheep consume the grain and hay, their usefulness will be ended," Loomis pointed out. "We can dine on the extra mutton."

"I still say we should make a dash for it," Owenby argued. "We could be to the border in four or five more days."

"He'd overtake us in the open," Loomis told him. "The landforms on that route dip below nine thousand feet. We'd lose all advantage."

"We won't be safe at the Indian border," Khalde said. "Oztrak will follow us on across the border into India. Borders mean nothing to him."

The Kamala Lama picked up the map and studied it. He traced Loomis's markings with a forefinger.

"This route has been used many times before," he said. "At least in legend. The Buddhist monk Hsüan-tsang went from China early in the seventh century. His journey has been the basis for dramatic treatment ever since. The most famous, of course, was the novel by Wu Ch'eng-en in the sixteenth century. I believe it was translated into English as *The Journey to the West.*"

"I've heard of it," Owenby said. "Seen it in the shops. But I've never read it."

"Hsüan-tsang's pilgrimage has been dramatized in song, dance, operas, and theater," the lama went on. "His companion, Sun Wu-k'ung, is one of the most popular figures in Chinese folklore."

"The monkey trickster," Lhalde said. "An apprentice

monk. He encountered dragons, the white tiger, the cadaver monster—all sorts of obnoxious creatures. I hope we fare better."

"Oztrak is obnoxious enough for me," Owenby said.

"I enjoy the myth," said the Kalmala Lama. "But it's the historical Hsüan-tsang who interests me most. He spent sixteen years of study in India. He returned with some of the texts we now must rescue from oblivion."

"Thirteen centuries later," Khalde said.

"We may find some of his experiences on the journey useful," the lama said. "I'll try to keep them in mind."

"Hsüan-tsang made his pilgrimage with experienced travelers," Khalde said. "Some of our monks are aged. With the altitude and the added hardship of winter, I fear some may not survive the journey."

Loomis and the Kamala Lama exchanged glances. Loomis remembered the lama's admonition that the safety of the manuscripts came before any consideration of lives.

"We'll do the best we can for them," Loomis promised. "And if anyone has an alternate plan, I'd be happy to hear it."

No one responded. For a time the silence was broken only by the murmur of the wind-whipped fire and the subdued camp sounds.

"Then it appears we're stuck with this one," Loomis said. "Tomorrow morning we'll head northwest, toward the high country."

Oztrak brought out his compass once more to confirm his direction of travel. Again he could hardly believe the result. Why had Loomis turned toward the northwest?

Bone-weary and half frozen, he shifted his weight in the saddle, trying to revive circulation to his feet. He and his men had not stopped for seven hours. Light snow had been falling through the last four—fortunately not enough to cover the tracks of Loomis and his caravan.

Oztrak pulled his map from beneath his sheepskin coat and steadied it against the saddle.

He could not find a single safe refuge for Loomis and Khalde in that direction. Ahead, over distant mountain ranges, lay Jammu and Kashmir, both battling for independence, their lands hotly disputed among the overlapping claims of China, Afghanistan, India, and Pakistan. If Loomis dared to cross into that region, he and his monks might be considered armed invaders and shot on sight. Oztrak could not fathom Loomis's destination or his reason for traveling in this direction. He hated mysteries.

He summoned Kiyak.

"How are the men faring?" he asked.

Kiyak raised his face hood to speak. "They're exhausted and cold, my commander. A brief rest would do both men and horses much good."

"We can't stop," Oztrak told him. "But you can spread my words. We are close behind the enemy. Tell the men the yak droppings are fresh, no more than four hours old."

"Begging your pardon, my commander. Our trackers say eight to twelve hours."

Oztrak was irritated. Kiyak tended to question orders. He lacked much-needed discipline.

"In this weather who can tell with any certainty?" Oztrak said. "Make it four."

Again Kiyak pulled his face covering aside. "Yes, my commander."

"And let's step up the pace. The enemy can't be far ahead of us."

Kiyak acknowledged and rode back to pass the word to the squadron commanders. Oztrak lashed his horse with the free end of his reins, prodding him into longer strides.

They were traveling through flat country, devoid of grass and other vegetation. Here and there a low outcropping of rock provided the only landmarks. The heavy overcast hid the distant mountain ranges shown on the map.

Oztrak noticed that his horse was laboring, breathing

hard even at a walk. The land sloped steadily upward. Oztrak assumed his horse was experiencing difficulty because they were climbing a moderate grade.

Twice during the next hour he thought he saw movement on the horizon. But each time he concluded that he had been mistaken. The wind was causing his eyes to water. He assumed that this was affecting his vision.

As he lashed his horse once more, a shout came from somewhere behind him. Oztrak glanced back.

A horse was down, its rider partially pinned. Several of the man's comrades quickly dismounted to help.

Irritated, Oztrak raised a hand, bringing his army to a halt. He assumed it to be a minor incident, that in a moment he could resume the march.

But quickly another horse went down—and another. Panic seemed to spread through all the horses. Within a minute, more than twenty were down, chests bellowing, eyes wide with fright.

Oztrak rode back to learn the cause.

Kiyak dismounted to examine two of the fallen horses. He remounted and came to meet Oztrak.

"This morning all the horses were fed from the barley we took from the *drokba,*" he said. "The *drokba* must have poisoned the grain."

But suddenly Oztrak knew.

"No, my young man. It isn't the grain. The horses are sick from the altitude. I've experienced this difficulty before, during a campaign against the Soviet invaders in northern Afghanistan."

Even as he spoke, another horse sank to the ground. The rider fought in vain to make the horse rise.

"We'll stop here for a brief rest," he said. "Bring in the extra horses. Assign three horses to each man, to be ridden in rotation. Each man will be responsible for distributing the workload among his horses."

"Most of the extra horses are carrying packs," Kiyak pointed out.

"Throw out all excess baggage," Oztrak ordered.

"Tents, cooking equipment, camp gear. Keep only the grain and essentials."

In the next half hour Kiyak carried out Oztrak's orders. But it was found that twelve of the fallen horses suffered ruptured lungs. They had to be shot.

Oztrak made another difficult decision. He sensed that morale among his troops was again plummeting. While the men had pledged their lives to the *jihad,* they had not pledged the lives of their horses. Oztrak spoke to Kiyak.

"The men need rest," he conceded. "Tell them they can sleep four hours. We'll post only a minimal guard. No one will surprise us out here."

Oztrak submitted to the luxury of his field tent one last time before it was discarded. He ordered a fire and gradually warmed the numbness from his face and limbs.

He lay for a time on his sheepskin bed, but sleep would not come. He kept pondering the question: Why had Loomis suddenly turned and made a beeline toward the northwest, away from Nepal, away from India?

Again Oztrak unfolded his map. He studied it several minutes before seeing a pattern: Loomis was traversing the highest ground available.

Oztrak drew a line tracing Loomis's route. Every minor alteration that Loomis had made in his course was toward higher elevations. Plainly Loomis was utilizing portions of the high plateau where horses could not easily go.

Oztrak admired the tactic. Loomis was proving himself to be an especially resourceful opponent. But where was he headed? Oztrak contemplated the possibilities.

Afghanistan?

That seemed unlikely. The country had not yet recovered from its long war. Its people still suffered from a shortage of food and supplies. The population was mostly Muslim. Loomis's Buddhists would find no refuge there.

Pakistan?

Again, not likely. Pakistan was on the verge of war

with India. An armed caravan crossing its borders would be regarded with suspicion and probably hostility.

Kashmir and Jammu?

In that region borders were indistinct. A United Nations attempt to form a plebiscite had failed. At any turn Loomis might find himself confronted by guerrillas, elements of the Red army of China or troops from India.

After eliminating every other possibility, Oztrak was left with Nepal and India. But both lay in the opposite direction from Loomis's present course.

Oztrak considered Nepal. To get there Loomis would have to make a 180-degree turn and more or less retrace his route from the opposite direction. Crossing Tibet, he would encounter the roads, run the risk of encountering a Red army patrol. He might even be spotted by Chinese military planes. In that barren country, a three-hundred-fifty-man caravan with hundreds of yaks and sheep would be impossible to hide.

So once again Oztrak was left with India as Loomis's most probable destination. India long had been receptive to Tibetan refugees. There resided the Tibetan government in exile, headed by the Dalai Lama. And there Buddhism had thrived for two thousand years. From any consideration, India remained Loomis's most logical destination.

On the map, Oztrak traced Loomis's probable route to India, utilizing the highest elevations of the plateau.

After making a loop to the northwest, Loomis could reach India over high ground by turning almost straight south, traveling along Tibet's western border.

The more Oztrak pondered the route, the more certain he became that this was Loomis's plan. Nothing else in Loomis's erratic route made sense.

Apparently Loomis had taken this route as a diversion, to hide his true destination, and—most especially—to eliminate pursuit by overtaxing Oztrak's horses.

Carefully, Oztrak plotted a course from his present position to Loomis's probable route south.

By traveling southwest, he might be able to intercept

Loomis on his way south, after his long loop to the northwest. This route to an interception would be half the distance Loomis would travel. More important, the route adhered to much lower terrain. If he took that course, he could travel more leisurely, and not overtax his horses.

The risk was high. Loomis might have another destination in mind. The region where Oztrak hoped to intercept him was vast. The odds against finding Loomis in that barren country were high.

Oztrak considered his options. He found only three.

He could abandon the chase and return to Turpan empty-handed. That option was totally unacceptable.

He could continue on Loomis's trail and follow him into the even higher elevations ahead. That, too, was unacceptable.

Or he could cut across to intercept Loomis's most probable route. Oztrak reasoned that by spreading a net of patrols, he could increase the odds of finding Loomis.

It would be a desperate gamble. But after thinking the matter through thoroughly, Oztrak felt he had no choice.

He ordered the squadrons awakened. He summoned them into formation. He mounted his horse, faced them in the wind and cold, and raised his voice.

"Allah has been kind," he shouted. "I have received today a revelation on where to find our enemy. We will abandon this trail, go there and wait for him. I have promised you a victory. You shall have it. Long live the *jihad!*"

The first response was weak. Only a few voices began the customary chant. But that first glimmer of enthusiasm soon fed on itself. Within a minute every man was shouting his praise to Allah.

Oztrak turned to Kiyak.

"Have the cooks prepare a feast," he ordered. "We'll spend the night here and restore our bodies and souls. Tomorrow, we'll put Allah's new plan into motion."

16

Loomis grew increasingly worried. Khedru and his six-man reconnaissance patrol had been out forty-eight hours. His instructions were to drop back until he caught sight of Oztrak, then to return immediately. Loomis was beginning to fear they might have been slain or, worse, captured.

Loomis tugged his heavily quilted cap lower and scraped ice from his face mask. He was stiff from his knees-under-chin riding posture on the yak.

All day the caravan had pushed on toward the northwest in the face of wind-driven snow and sleet. Loomis was aware that the pace and high altitudes were taking a toll on both animals and men. Eleven of the older monks were seriously ill, four in critical condition.

Around him the caravan moved quietly, the normal sounds softened by mud and snow. The temperature was well below zero on the Farenheit scale. Here and there fresh droppings from the yaks and sheep steamed briefly in the icy wind.

Many of the monks were now on foot, leading their thirst-starved yaks, sparing them the additional suffering of carrying a rider. Only a few monks were still in the saddles. Zampo and the other elderly, ill monks were bundled in large baskets, strapped to the backs of the sturdier yaks. The Kamala Lama also was under heavy wraps in a covered palanquin borne by four plodding yaks. Six of his personal guard of warrior monks walked beside him.

The caravan was stretched almost a half mile. With the sheep herd, it ranged almost two hundred yards wide. Despite the efforts of the tenders, the sheep tended to bunch up and knock their packs together. Only wider freedom of movement seemed to relieve the situation.

Lhalde rode up beside Loomis. He turned his head and shouted against the wind.

"Zampo is dying, Mr. Loomis. I hope we can stop for a few minutes. Build a fire. Let him die in warmth."

Loomis opened his mouth to deny the request, but immediately reconsidered. Thus far he had seen no sign of pursuit. He felt he had gained some advantage with the higher terrain. If danger still lay ahead, the men and animals should be in good condition.

And perhaps a brief stop would give Khedru and his patrol time to catch up. Zampo was one hundred and two years old. Khalde's request was reasonable: Zampo deserved to spend his last moments in this life in warmth and comfort.

"We can stop here till morning," Loomis said. "We can melt snow and water the livestock, give them extra grain. We're almost to the point where we turn south. From there we should try for better speed."

"I'm most grateful for your consideration," Lhalde said. He turned and rode back to where several monks were walking beside the yak bearing the ill Zampo.

Word was passed. The caravan stopped. Lean-to shelters were erected and fires built.

Loomis and Owenby organized a production line among the monks, scooping up snow, bringing it to the fires for melting, and rushing the water to the yaks and sheep before it again froze.

While the livestock was watered and fed, other monks prepared food for the camp.

Loomis posted a double guard, concerned that a proper defense would be impossible in this open terrain.

He found himself eager for the turn south and the broken country that lay in that direction, where his smaller force could be used to better advantage.

Before turning in, he made a brief inspection tour of the camp. The yaks and sheep, held in separate herds, were huddled together for protection against the wind. A knot of monks stood quietly keeping vigil at the shelter where Zampo lay dying. Zampo's precious manuscripts were stored safely under their own shelter.

Satisfied that all was well, Loomis crawled into his bedroll for a few hours of sleep.

A short time later Owenby awakened him.

"Sorry to interrupt your beauty nap, but Khedru and his patrol just came in. They have some interesting news. I thought you'd want to know."

Loomis pulled on his boots and went to the fire where Khedru and his patrol were seated at a belated supper. All appeared to be on the ragged edge of complete exhaustion. Loomis squatted by the fire and helped himself to hot tea.

Khedru was talking. Owenby was listening, offering occasional comment.

At last Owenby gave Loomis a summary.

"He says they dropped back twenty-five or thirty kilometers after leaving us. There they waited a full day before Oztrak and his men showed. The buggers were having trouble with their horses. Two dozen or more went down. A few were shot. That night the Uighurs tossed a bloody feast. The next morning, they gave up and turned back."

Loomis found that difficult to believe.

"What direction did they take?"

Owenby queried Khedru at length.

"He swears they went back the same way they came.

Makes sense, once you stop to think about it. What the hell else could he do? Continue on? Leave his men afoot in this godforsaken country? Not bloody likely. I think we're done with the bastard."

Loomis was skeptical. He thought of the repeated, fanatic, costly charges against the barricade. He remembered the utter cruelty in the murders of Lhalde's three monks. These were not people who gave up.

"Did Khedru follow them?"

"He says there was no need. He could see them for twenty kilometers."

"And they rode exactly back over their own tracks? Question him on this point. It's important."

Again Owenby spoke with Khedru at length.

"He says they may have turned a slight bit to the south. He thinks they were heading toward lower ground as fast as possible because of the horses."

Loomis was not comfortable with the theory. As yet he did not know why.

"How many men does Oztrak have left?"

Owenby asked Khedru, who answered at length.

"He estimates about three hundred, maybe a few more. But the bugger still has about a thousand horses. Every man jack of his was riding one, leading two. So they must have been spelling off the horses. And even so they couldn't cut it."

Loomis brought out his map. Khedru pinpointed the spot where the Uighurs were last seen.

Loomis searched to the south on the map. The contour lines confirmed that the shortest route to lower ground lay in that direction.

He checked his own position. From the turning point tomorrow, his route would be a straight shot south, four hundred kilometers to the Himalayas and the border of India.

"I think we can ease up a bit now, old sod," Owenby said. "Have you noticed? Our bloody yaks are down to skin and bone. They won't make India at this pace."

That was true. Some of the yaks were terribly gaunt.

But Loomis could not believe that Oztrak had given up. He felt that somehow he knew the man's mind.

"We can't risk letting up until we're over the Himalayas," Loomis told him. "Hard traveling may cost us some of the livestock. But not all."

"We've lost Oztrak. So what's the bloody point?"

"I doubt we've lost him. Tell Khedru that beginning tomorrow we'll move most of our rear guard to the front. I'll go over details with him in the morning."

Lhalde came to join them at the fire. Loomis caught the glint of tears in the old monk's eyes. He spoke to Khedru and his men in Tibetan, then turned to Loomis.

"Zampo just passed on," he said.

The news affected Khedru and his men profoundly. Immediately they left the fire and joined the monks around Zampo's body. A few moments later a steady chanting came from the lean-to. Loomis assumed they were reciting prayers for the dead.

"We'll bury him in the morning," Lhalde said to Loomis. "I trust we can spare time for a brief ceremony."

"Of course," Loomis said.

"A hundred and two years old," Owenby said. "Then to be buried in a barren pile of rocks like this. It doesn't seem right."

Lhalde answered so quietly that Loomis almost missed his words.

"Zampo has seen worse," he said.

Owenby looked at Loomis and rolled his eyes skyward.

The ceremony the next morning was conducted in driving sleet. Lhalde said that normally the rituals would have continued for at least two days and perhaps the better part of a week. But they dispensed with Zampo in less than thirty minutes.

A short time later the caravan turned south. Loomis put flankers out, with six warrior monks riding point. Only three men were left as rear guard, to give the alarm if pursuit was sighted.

As they moved south the wind continued to howl out

of the north, but the snow and sleet became intermittent. Since they no longer were climbing, travel became easier. The conditions of the ill monks showed improvement. The mood of the entire caravan rose.

"I think we've bloody well done it," Owenby declared. "After what we've been through, a little stroll over the Himalayas should be a breeze."

Loomis did not answer. He kept remembering the theory of the Kamala Lama that old enemies meet again in every lifetime to renew ancient battles.

He remained convinced that his encounter with Oztrak had yet to reach a resolution. He could not shake the feeling that the final confrontation—at least in this lifetime—still lay ahead.

Riding sixty feet to the front of the squadrons, Oztrak and Kiyak were first to reach the crest of the hill. They were met by a renewed onslaught of icy wind and sleet. Ahead, across a wide, shallow valley, lay yet another grass-mantled hill.

Oztrak suppressed a curse. It had been the same for six hours now, one hill after another.

"I don't understand this," he admitted to Kiyak. "The map shows this as a massive ridge, not hills and valleys."

"Maybe we're not there yet," Kiyak said. "Maybe the ridge lies farther on."

"We're now on the highest ground," Oztrak said. "This is the top of the ridge. It was wrong of me to assume that the ridge would be level on top."

Accustomed to desert and plain, Oztrak also had assumed he would be able to keep watch over vast distances. But in this gently undulating landscape, the horizon often was less than a kilometer away, and now even that was obscured by snow and a lowering overcast. Loomis could bring his entire caravan down any one of dozens of valleys and pass unseen.

Oztrak was distressed by the unexpected difficulty. In order to keep watch across the entire ridge, he must devise a plan to utilize every resource of his command.

His map showed the ridge as averaging fifteen miles wide. He calculated that he now was about halfway across.

"We'll camp here," he said. "The enemy will pass within seven miles of this spot. From here we will spread out a net to catch him."

He waited until lean-to shelters were erected against the wind and sleet and fires built before summoning Kiyak and the squadron commanders and outlining his plan.

"Beginning now, we'll send out two-man patrols, east and west, every fifteen minutes. Each patrol will go out ten miles, turn, and retrace the route back to camp. The patrols must maintain the interval between them at all times. The enemy must not get past them. The first patrol to sight the enemy or his tracks will ride back at a gallop to meet the patrol immediately behind. The word will be conveyed from patrol to patrol. In this way the report can be brought to us in relays as fast as possible."

Kiyak proved he had a quick mind. "This plan will require one hundred sixty men on patrol at all times, my commander. Eighty in each direction."

Oztrak accepted the calculation with a nod. "The remainder of the squadrons will remain on alert, prepared to take to the field within five minutes, day or night."

The squadron commanders exchanged glances. Guven, the oldest of the three, cleared his throat hesitantly.

"My commander, the men are very tired. They haven't yet grown accustomed to this high country. I feel I should point out that the long patrols in this weather and the constant state of readiness will be extremely detrimental to their fighting efficiency."

Oztrak gave Guven a lengthy, silent stare. Guven had the grace to blush.

"The enemy is almost within our grasp," Oztrak told him. "There can be no rest now. Only after the enemy is eliminated will we rest. Is that understood?"

Guven nodded. "Yes, my commander."

"Then please follow my orders without argument."

The first two patrols went out immediately. Like clockwork, two more patrols followed every quarter hour.

Oztrak soon became aware of grumbling around the camp. His young volunteers had pledged their lives to the *jihad* with visions of thrilling cavalry charges and hand-to-hand combat. None was prepared for the dull, grinding hardship of life in the field.

The complaints grew even more vocal after the first patrols returned, exhausted and half frozen from long exposure to the wind. As the days passed, Oztrak felt sullen eyes upon him. He knew the tenor of his men's thinking: If Allah had truly provided a revelation, why could He not have been more specific? Why do we have to endure these long patrols?

In truth, Oztrak's own spirits also reached a new low. He had expected to intercept Loomis on the second day, or perhaps the third. But four days went by without sign of him.

Oztrak became plagued by doubt. Had Loomis gone on north, into Jammu and Kashmir? Oztrak could not rule out the possibility. Loomis had shown a talent for the unexpected.

He began to fear that Loomis might have tricked him one more time.

On the evening of the fourth day, Kiyak came to him with a strange, diffident manner.

"My commander, two of our men have disappeared. Hizel and Sakman."

Oztrak's first thought was that they had encountered the enemy and were taken captive.

"Disappeared? How?"

Kiyak seemed reluctant to speak. "They were on patrol, my commander. When they reached the point where the patrols normally turn back, they kept on riding. Earlier they were seen stuffing their saddlebags with food. It is believed they are riding toward home."

"The fools!" Oztrak exploded.

He doubted either man had sufficient brains to find his way home. He thought of the ramifications: This could be the start of widespread desertions.

"Kiyak, I want you to attend to this personally," he said. "Take ten men and go after them. Bring them back to me, dead or alive.

Kiyak's hesitation was almost imperceptible. Almost.

"It will be done, my commander."

Kiyak was gone twelve hours. Just before noon on the following day he returned with Hizel and Sakman.

Oztrak ordered all the men not on patrol into formation to witness punishment. Hizel and Sakman were brought before him, their hands bound behind them.

Oztrak raised his voice so every man in camp could hear.

"You two pigs have broken your sacred vows to Allah. The penalty is death. Do you have anything to say before the penalty is enacted?"

Hizel and Sakman stood mute with shock. For a brief moment Oztrak was touched by their youth. They were no more than seventeen. Both had attempted beards, but the result was hardly more than scraggly fuzz.

Oztrak stood awaiting their reply. Sakman's mouth worked tentatively, but no words came.

Oztrak unsheathed his sword. Hizel and Sakman stared at it as if in a dream. Oztrak placed the tip of the sword on Sakman's right shoulder.

"Allah gave you life. Now Allah takes away your life," Oztrak said.

He pulled back the sword and swung the blade with all his strength. Sakman's head popped into the air fully two hand spans above the severed neck, then fell to earth with the sound of a dropped melon. The body, spewing a fountain of blood and froth, collapsed at Oztrak's feet.

Oztrak heard men vomiting in the ranks. He ignored them.

Hizel dodged his head like a chicken. But Oztrak was too quick for him. Hizel's head fell beside Sakman's. The two bodies continued to jerk in the dirt several seconds, then lay still.

Oztrak drew a white handkerchief from his coat and wiped the blood off his sword. He then faced his command.

"You have witnessed the penalty for those who forget their sacred vows to Allah. Praise be to Allah!"

He turned to Kiyak, whose face was remarkably pale. "Dismiss the command."

Oztrak returned to his lean-to shelter with the first feeling of satisfaction he had experienced in days. He did not know yet if he would find Loomis. But he was certain there would be no more desertions in his command.

17

During the night the sky cleared and at dawn the Zaskar Mountains, frontal range of the Himalayas, stood before them like a single, massive piece of carved jade. Loomis estimated the distance at forty miles.

All morning the caravan moved steadily toward the mountains, traveling along a shallow valley near the crest of the ridge. The flankers rode along the tops of the hills on each side. The yaks led the caravan, carrying monks and the precious cargo of manuscripts. The sheep were close behind, plodding along at their own pace. Loomis glanced back. His rear guard trailed the sheep by a quarter of a mile.

Toward noon Lhalde came to ride beside Loomis and Owenby. Despite his age, Lhalde kept close watch over the caravan. Under his guidance, the monks continued their *vinaya*—system of monastic discipline—even while covering ground and tending to all their duties.

Ahead, waving golden grass and patches of blinding white snow provided a proper setting for the mountains.

"Beautiful sight," Lhalde observed as their yaks walked along side by side.

"You've been this way before, I take it," Owenby said. "Other lives, I mean."

Lhalde smiled, aware that Owenby, a skeptic, was needling him.

"Actually, no," he said. "The traditional way to India has always been across the Gobi Desert, then south over the Hindu Kush into Peshawar—now in Pakistan. That's the route the monk Hsüan-tsang took in the seventh century in his *Journey to the West.* The way we're going has been used by us only the last thousand years or so."

"What route did your trickster monkey-monk go?" Owenby asked.

Lhalde took no offense. Again he smiled.

"The majority of scholars agree most landmarks in Wu Ch'eng-en's novel were allegorical. The fanciful names have been applied to various places. But actual attribution is risky."

Loomis had gathered that Lhalde and the Kamala Lama considered the manuscripts of Hsüan-tsang among the most valuable in the library. Their passion on the subject had made him curious.

"What knowledge did Hsüan-tsang bring back from India?" he asked.

Lhalde gave Loomis a quick glance to make certain his interest was genuine. Apparently he judged it was.

"Hsüan-tsang brought back more than thirteen hundred volumes of the rarest and most ancient of Buddhist liturgical texts. He translated seventy-three of those volumes before he died. But most important were his own writings on what he learned. That principally is the focus of our collection—his discoveries in his search for knowledge about Buddhism."

Loomis wondered whether Hsüan-tsang's writings were truly important or whether Lhalde and the Kamala Lama were merely caught up in their own enthusiasm. The writings of an obscure seventh-century monk hardly seemed comparable with the lost letters of the Apostle Paul.

"Why are Hsüan-tsang's writings so important?" he asked. "What did he discover?"

Lhalde gave Loomis another analytical glance.

"Hsüan-tsang long had been concerned over discrepancies he perceived in the Buddhist thinking of his day, which held that there was no self in nirvana. So he went to India to find the fundamental texts of Buddhism. From them he concluded that the final state of nirvana is one of bliss and purity in the eternal self. His conclusions are important because his findings penetrate the complete underlying foundation of Buddhism. From his extensive scholarship he founded a belief that all living beings possess the Buddha nature, that all beings from the beginning of time have participated in the Buddha's eternal existence and may achieve the goal of spiritual union with Buddha."

Loomis studied the distant mountains. At odd moments the landscape, the rituals of Buddhism seemed to acquire a disturbing familiarity. He could not forget the Kamala Lama's discourse on the subject.

"What will happen to the manuscripts after we get to India?" he asked.

"They'll be preserved in the new lamasery we will build there. I anticipate that our collection of Hsüan-tsang's writings will inspire a revival of Buddhism, perhaps in the form of a new school of thought. Quietly, we'll also confide to Christians, Jews, Hindus, Taoists, other religions what we possess. Conceivably what we're carrying could instigate a reawakening in all faiths. But for that to happen conditions must be receptive. If this doesn't occur in the near future, it will later. We're not concerned about when. As long as the truth exists, the potential is always there."

The tranquillity of the caravan—and of the conversation—was shattered by a shout from one of the flankers. Loomis looked up just in time to see two riders wheel their horses and disappear back over the top of the hill.

The riders had accorded the caravan only a glimpse of them. But for Loomis it was enough.

"What the bloody hell?" Owenby said.

The flankers lashed their yaks and rode over the hill in a fruitless effort to keep the fleeing horsemen in sight.

"Oztrak's men?" Owenby asked.

"I'm certain of it," Loomis said.

"They might have been local nomads," Khalde said. "Some of the *drokba* have horses."

"Both of those men had rifles," Loomis pointed out. "If they were nomads, why did they run?"

Lhalde did not answer.

Loomis considered his situation. Apparently Oztrak had seen through his ploy of keeping to the high ground and had turned southwest to intercept him. If so, Oztrak probably had sent patrols out all along the ridge and the two men were now dashing back to report their sighting.

The distance to Oztrak's main body of men posed the crucial question. How long would it take for the two riders to reach Oztrak and for Oztrak to get his troops organized?

If the caravan was attacked here on the ridge, defense would be almost impossible. The low, undulating hills offered no protection, no place to make a stand.

Loomis knew he should put as much ground between the caravan and Oztrak as possible.

"Quick," Loomis said to Lhalde. "Get the caravan moving all-out."

Lhalde turned and dashed down the length of the caravan, spreading the word. The yaks began moving forward at a trot.

"We can't hope to outrun the buggers," Owenby pointed out.

"I know," Loomis said. "But we've got to find a better defensive position than this."

"And if we don't?"

"We'll turn and fight the best we can," Loomis said. "There's nothing else we can do."

* * *

It was a problem of logistics. Oztrak's men were spread out over fifteen miles. He could not reassemble them immediately. Should he leave without them?

Loomis had been sighted five miles to the east. Even now he no doubt was making a dash for the mountains.

Oztrak weighed the advantages and disadvantages and decided he had no time to waste in getting his army together.

"We'll go after the enemy with what we have," he told Kiyak. "The men on patrol can assemble here and follow us as soon as they're able."

Oztrak was not at all happy with the situation. One hundred forty-six of his men were out on patrol. He was leaving camp with less than half of his remaining army.

For five days horses had been kept saddled, girths loose. The men had slept with rifles by their sides. Now they only had to tighten the girths, step into the saddle, and they were ready to ride.

They hurried east at a brisk trot, each man riding one horse and leading two. Oztrak was tempted to set a faster pace, but he did not know how lengthy a chase lay ahead. He felt he should conserve the horses as much as possible.

The landscape ahead was breathtaking. The front range of the Himalayas lay on the southern horizon like a protective cloud. Oztrak had known all along that the mountains were there, only forty miles away. But while hidden by mists, clouds, snow, and rain, their presence had been only theoretical.

Now, plainly visible, they posed a clear and immediate hazard. If Loomis managed to reach them, his destruction would be far more difficult.

In a little more than an hour Oztrak reached the place where Loomis had been sighted. He rode down into the shallow valley and examined the abundance of tracks.

As he had anticipated, Loomis was heading straight toward the mountains.

Oztrak rode back to the head of his column.

"Forward at a gallop," he ordered.

"My commander, the horses are laboring," Kiyak said. "If we overtax them, they'll fail us."

For a moment Oztrak was consumed by blind fury. He considered hitting his second-in-command with the flat of his sword. Oztrak never tolerated the slightest questioning of his orders.

"Young man, if we kill the horses, so be it," Oztrak said. "We'll finish the job on foot."

"But it isn't necessary to lose the horses, my commander. We'll catch the enemy soon enough at a trot. There's no possibility of his escape."

"Convey my order!" Oztrak shouted. "I assure you, if we don't catch the enemy before he reaches the mountains, the horses won't be the only ones to suffer."

Kiyak turned and issued the order.

Oztrak battled his anger as they rode on south. Almost a half hour passed before the first horse collapsed. Again it was as if a panic swept through the herd. Within minutes more than a dozen were down screaming, flailing on the ground.

"Shoot the fallen horses," Oztrak shouted to Kiyak. "Tell the men not to bother transferring saddles. We can retrieve them later."

After another hour more than half the men were riding bareback. But lightened of saddles and other soldierly trappings, the horses labored less. Despite the distance traveled, fewer collapsed.

Gradually the terrain changed. From the gently undulating grasslands, the landscape became broken and studded with scattered boulders. The mountains now seemed much nearer, jade green against a deep blue sky.

Oztrak stood in his saddle and peered ahead. He still could not see the enemy. He glanced back. While coping with their fallen horses, many of his men had fallen a considerable distance behind. This would never do.

"Order those men to close up," he shouted to Kiyak. "We may come upon the enemy at any moment."

But the minutes crept by and still they caught no glimpse of the enemy. More horses collapsed. Disorder became even worse in the column.

Oztrak knew his command was strung out all the way back to the base camp, now fifteen miles away.

He faced another crucial decision. If he stopped to put his men into some semblance of order, more valuable time would be lost. Yet, after past experiences, he felt it inadvisable to come upon this enemy piecemeal.

Oztrak was considering the alternatives when one of his point men leaned from the saddle and plucked a yak dropping from the ground. He laughed as he squeezed the manure through his fingers.

"Less than half an hour old, my commander," he shouted. "We're almost upon them."

Oztrak made his decision. If he alone caught up with the enemy, he would engage and delay Loomis until the rest of the army arrived.

"Faster!" he shouted to Kiyak. "Loomis must not reach the mountains!"

18

"We can't keep this up," Owenby shouted to Loomis. "We're killing the bloody yaks."

Loomis nodded. He was aware of the situation. Most of the yaks could not last much longer.

The caravan was climbing a steep rise. The yaks heaved noisily from the exertion, nostrils flaring, their necks and flanks flecked with foamy sweat. The monks clung to the backs of their mounts with the intensity of exhausted, desperate men. Only the sheep seemed to relish the pace. They skittered along bunched, making occasional leaps.

Loomis searched ahead for the geology he sought. Although the ground was more broken, only the occasional small boulders offered protection.

The mountains now seemed to hang over the caravan, tantalizingly close, yet beyond immediate reach. They rose like solid wall. Passage through them appeared impossible. But Loomis had studied the ancient maps unearthed by Zampo before the evacuation of the lamasery. The hand-drawn maps detailed a tortuous route through many passes, leading over what was labeled "the backbone of the world."

Loomis topped a rise and studied the ground ahead. To his great relief, the landscape offered the first hint of the type of terrain he sought: Shards of broken strata lay among the boulders. On each side sheer bluffs rose, forming a deep gorge. A small stream snaked along beside the trail.

The next climb was steep. A few of the yaks staggered in making their way up the climb. Owenby looked back at Loomis in a silent plea.

"Only a little farther," Loomis shouted to him.

They crossed into another valley and climbed the next hill. Tailings from exposed strata grew more numerous.

As he reached the crest of the next hill, Loomis knew at first glance he had found his defensive position.

The site exceeded all his expectations. The valley ahead formed a large bowl, broken only by the downward course of the small stream and the trail beside it. Loomis recognized the geology. In the formation of the mountain range, subterranean limestone had been shattered and uplifted by the intense pressures. The broken shards of strata had been pushed to the surface. They lay exposed in huge slabs standing on end. The opposite slope resembled the giant statuary on Easter Island.

"This is it," Loomis shouted to Owenby. "Get Khedru and his men together. And bring Drupa."

In the narrow confines of the gorge the caravan was strung out more than a half mile. Loomis rode to the head of the caravan to confer hurriedly with Lhalde.

"Take the caravan on into the mountains as far as you can go without stopping," Loomis said. "We'll fight a delaying action here, then pull back and come in behind you."

"The maps indicate a difficult climb five or six miles ahead," Lhalde reminded him. "The yaks badly need rest. I don't feel we should start up that portion of the trail until we can do it rapidly."

Loomis understood Lhalde's point. On the switchbacks of a steep climb, the caravan would be vulnerable to gunfire from below. Lhalde was asking for time to rest the yaks and to give them grain and water before starting up.

"You can stop there for a breather," Loomis agreed. "We'll hold Oztrak here as long as we can. But don't stop too long. An hour or two at most. When you start up, abandon the weaker yaks, if you must. Don't let them hold you back."

The palanquin of the Kamala Lama was close enough that he overheard the exchange. He pushed aside the curtains.

"Mr. Loomis, I trust you'll bear in mind the priorities I mentioned in our first talk. In keeping with that request, I believe it's time I relinquished my personal bodyguards. You may need them here."

Loomis considered the suggestion. Khedru had assigned six of the warrior monks to accompany the lama at all times. True, Loomis needed them in forming his line of defense. But he could not be certain the caravan itself would escape attack.

Although Loomis had seen no evidence, Oztrak could have sent a detachment into the mountains ahead of everyone. Even now they might be lying in wait somewhere up ahead.

"We should have some warriors with the caravan," Loomis told the Kamala Lama. "If an emergency arises, we'll hear their rifle fire and fall back immediately to join you. That way the library will be protected."

The lama nodded in recognition of the logic.

"I keep thinking all the danger is pursuing us," he said. "But you're right. The danger may be anywhere."

Loomis hurried back to where Owenby, Khedru, Drupa, and the warrior monks were assembled beside the small stream.

"We don't have much time," Loomis told Owenby. "Tell the men we'll hold the Uighurs here while the caravan goes on into the mountains. Then we'll fall back by the numbers, exactly the way we did in front of the lamasery on that last day. Ask them if everyone understands."

Loomis waited patiently while Owenby translated. No one raised a question.

"Tell Khedru to assign someone to hold our yaks just over the next hill," Loomis continued. "Tell Drupa to stay with the yaks and to be ready with explosives and detonators. Each time we fall back, we may mine the trail."

Owenby conveyed the order to Drupa, who nodded to show he understood. Three of the yaks were loaded with the last of his explosives. He had utilized some in making more bamboo claymores, but most of the blasting powder remained in bulk form.

"Tell the men that I'll assign each to a position," Loomis said. "They're to stay out of sight until I give the signal by opening fire. Then they can start shooting. Stress that they're to shoot to kill. They're to pop up, shoot, and duck out of sight again. Tell them to move around, so the Uighurs will never know where they'll pop up next. Tell them to take quick shots, never giving the Uighurs time to draw a bead."

Owenby talked for several minutes, explaining the tactics. The monks absorbed the instructions without expression and with total concentration. Loomis had not seen such dedicated soldiering since the early days of the Green Berets.

By the time Loomis finished with his instructions, the caravan had disappeared over the next hill. Hurriedly Loomis assigned the men, placing each behind one of the huge chunks of broken strata. The positions formed a half moon blocking the gorge and commanded an uninterrupted view of the trail below.

Ideally, Loomis also would have assigned men to the heights above to prevent flanking. But he had neither time nor a sufficient number of rifles.

With every man in place, Loomis moved to his own carefully chosen position on top of a twenty-foot-high chunk of limestone. The brief climb gave him a sweeping view of the trail below and of his own half-moon defense.

He utilized the old ninja trick of hiding in plain sight by resembling anything but a human body. Twisting into a pretzel shape, he pointed his rifle at the spot where he expected Oztrak and his men to appear.

Then he waited, motionless.

Several hours of daylight remained, but already the sun had passed over the snowcapped mountains to the west, leaving the gorge in shadow. Freezing temperatures persisted. The earlier breeze had died away to an unnatural stillness.

The long wait seemed interminable. Loomis worried that the warrior monks would grow stiff and numb lying motionless in the cold. The frozen stream, the calm air cast an unnatural aspect to the gorge. Loomis was familiar with the phenomenon; battles were always fought in a dreamlike setting.

At last, from beyond the hill, came the faint sounds of horses' hooves against stone, an occasional curse or command. Slowly the sounds grew in volume. Then the leading elements of Oztrak's army appeared at the crest of the hill.

First came a six-man squad riding point, led by a strikingly handsome young officer. For a moment Loomis thought he was the same man who had led the cavalry charges and the scaling of the north ridge. But at nearer range Loomis recognized that this was a different, even younger man, albeit a carbon copy, right down to the elaborate moustache and well-trimmed beard.

And this one was far more cautious. Every twenty yards or so he reined in and sat examining the trail ahead. Frequently he issued orders to his men, gesturing for them to spread out. He came on down into the gorge relentlessly but carefully. He and his squad were well in the advance. Although Loomis heard more Uighurs approaching, none had yet come over the top of the hill.

Patiently Loomis waited, determined to allow the

six-man squad to pass behind him if necessary. He wanted Oztrak and the main body of Uighurs well within range before the shooting began.

Forty yards away, the youth stopped for a longer interval, searching the trail ahead. Loomis doubted that the youth had seen anything to arouse his suspicions. But all his instincts for caution obviously were working.

Behind him, the first of the Uighur cavalry came into view. They rode tightly packed on the narrow trail, moving at a slow walk. Even from the distance Loomis observed that the horses were in poor condition.

Still the youth hesitated. Several times he looked right at Loomis. Each time Loomis felt his gaze linger, then move on.

After a time the youth apparently decided that Loomis was only another gnarled, stunted pine. He raised an arm and motioned his squad forward.

Loomis allowed the six-man squad to pass beneath him, trusting that they would continue to examine the trail ahead and fail to look back.

The cavalry continued its advance into the gorge. Loomis searched the faces, the positions of the riders, trying to determine which was Oztrak. But the cavalry lacked organization. No one seemed to be in charge.

Loomis waited for another squadron to come into view. None did.

The first group—no more than fifty men—apparently was traveling alone. Loomis held his fire until the forward element was no more than fifty yards away.

Still no more Uighurs appeared.

Loomis felt he could delay no longer. He selected a target—a rider who seemed older than the rest—and fired, knocking the man from the saddle. Instantly the warrior monks laid down a furious opening barrage.

Loomis did not wait to see the results. His concern was for the squad he had allowed to pass to the rear.

He turned on his perch. The young squad leader was in the open, thirty yards up the trail.

Loomis shot him.

The rest of the squad sought cover, but none made it. Loomis shot one. The monks cut down the other four.

Loomis returned his attention to the main body of cavalry. It was in full retreat, firing erratically as it went, leaving the dead and wounded behind.

Loomis joined in the firing, but soon the Uighurs were out of range. All shooting ceased.

Twenty-two bodies lay on the trail. Only two showed signs of life. Apparently the warrior monks were putting virtually every bullet in the ten ring. Their disciplined, intense concentration and many hours of dry-firing were now paying off.

From his high perch Loomis watched the sides of the gorge for any flanking movement. Owenby rose from his position behind an outcropping ten yards away.

"Well, we jolly well stopped them, old sod. What'll the buggers do now?"

Loomis was still puzzled over the unexpectedly small number of Uighurs. He could only guess at the reason.

The first theory that came to mind made sense.

"Oztrak will wait for reinforcements," he predicted. "Probably half his men were out on patrol when we were sighted. He didn't wait to gather them. Their horses are on their last legs. Some of the cavalry he left behind may be on foot."

"Let's hope," Owenby said. "Maybe that means we won't be on the shitty end of a cavalry charge."

"They wouldn't charge uphill anyway," Loomis said. "But we should be ready for them. Go check the positions. Make sure everyone understands what to expect."

Owenby left, running from one position to the next. Loomis continued to keep watch along the sides of the gorge. A few minutes later Owenby returned.

"We've one dead, but no wounded. Poor sod on the far end of the line got it right between the eyes. No one noticed till I found him."

Loomis winced. Attrition among his warrior monks was becoming critical. He now was down to twenty-six, plus the six with the caravan.

"If they come at us with three hundred men, we've had it," Owenby said. "So why don't we fall back? Maybe we could take them by surprise again."

Loomis thought of the steep climb ahead, the many switchbacks detailed on the ancient maps.

"We won't find another defensive position as good as this," Loomis told him. "We'll hold here as long as we're able."

"We have only two hours of daylight left," Oztrak said. "Loomis is delaying us so his caravan can make the climb over the pass five miles ahead. We must get past him quickly."

"It is impossible," said Erbakan, one of the new squadron commanders. "They are well hidden. When they shoot they never miss."

"You are a fool," Oztrak fumed. "Loomis is blocking our way with no more than thirty rifles. We have him outnumbered ten to one. You talk and fight like women! When we again attack, I want you and your squadron to roll right over the enemy."

Erbakan colored beneath his dark skin. "Begging your pardon, my commander. We lost twenty-eight brave men before we fell back. Not one fought like a woman."

"But you retreated," Oztrak pointed out. "A sprinkling of rifle fire and you fled."

They were gathered beside the trail, a hundred yards back from the top of the hill, waiting for the arrival of the second squadron. Oztrak was furious with the men, and he also was angry with himself. While he had gone back to put his stragglers into some semblance of order, he had allowed the inexperienced Kiyak to take the forward elements on into the mountains. Now he was down by another twenty-eight men.

"They have the way blocked, my commander," Erbakan said. "You'll see."

"Nonsense," Oztrak said. "We'll sweep them out of the way. I myself will lead you."

He estimated that two-thirds of his army had now arrived. Stragglers were still coming in.

He remembered the strange markings on the map detailing what lay ahead. First came the steep climb up to the first high pass. After that the trail snaked its way through the mountains in a series of passes, each higher than the last.

Once over the first pass, there would be no way to flank the Tibetans. His best course would be constant harassment, picking them off one by one in a running gun battle. There his superior numbers would make the difference.

But he still hoped such a long pursuit could be avoided. By overpowering Loomis now he would be able to catch the Tibetans exposed on the switchbacks ahead. There they would be like ducks in a shooting gallery.

Oztrak ordered a rifle and two bandoliers brought to him. Again he spoke to his squadron commanders.

"Now we will attack and push back the enemy," he said. "This is the way we will do it. We will put sharpshooters on the walls of the gorge to shoot down on them. We will move forward on foot, two hundred strong. We will crawl from boulder to boulder. We also will shoot from cover. Anyone can play that game."

19

Something moved up there," Owenby said. "Just to the right of those bloody bushes. See? There it is again."

Loomis grunted acknowledgment from his high perch. For several minutes he had been watching the Uighurs climb the sides of the gorge, wondering what he could do about it. They were still out of range.

"They're also crawling toward us through the grass and rocks," he said. "I could see them plain when they came over the hill. There's about two hundred of them."

"Jesus," Owenby said. "Then we've had it, haven't we?"

"Pass the word down the line that they're out there," Loomis said. "Tell them to open fire at any time on any clear target."

Owenby scurried away. Loomis shifted his position on his perch, bringing his rifle to bear on the side of the gorge where he had seen movement.

Owenby was right, of course. The monks could not hope to fight off two hundred Uighurs under these circumstances. For the first time since the long series of battles began, Loomis felt that the situation was out of his control. Until now he had always managed to contrive some advantage. Here he could find none.

A rifle fired to his left. Apparently one of the warrior monks had caught sight of a plain target. Other, scattered shots followed. Soon the shooting among the monks became general but sporadic.

The Uighurs held their fire, refusing to reveal their positions. Loomis sensed a new discipline among them. Earlier they had plunged headlong into every fight, taking every risk in stride. Now they kept to the safety of the grass and boulders, holding their fire. Loomis idly wondered if Oztrak himself had taken to the field, replacing his reckless senior officers.

A head and shoulders emerged high on the side of the gorge. Loomis drew a bead and fired. The Uighur lost his grip and tumbled down the steep slope. His body lodged against boulders and lay still.

Two bullets ricocheted off the rock beside Loomis, missing him by scant inches. He resumed fire, aiming at the muzzle flashes. Although he saw no sign that his shots took effect, the firing from that quarter ceased.

Below, the Uighurs in the grass at last opened fire, revealing their positions. The monks answered, and for several minutes the shooting became sustained.

More bullets struck near Loomis. They came from his right, somewhere on that wall of the gorge. Shooting also resumed on his left. For an uncomfortable minute he was caught in a crossfire. His cheek was stung by bits of rock, or perhaps of lead from a shattered bullet. He could not shoot in either direction without exposing himself to crossfire from the other. There was nothing else he could do but retreat.

He slid down the chunk of limestone. Owenby was lying flat, legs spaced, quartered to his target in military fashion. On hearing Loomis descending, he glanced up.

"Hot up there?" he asked. He performed a perfect double take. "You hit?"

Loomis felt a stream of blood coursing down his cheek. "Rock," he said.

Owenby raised up slightly to look out over the grass.

"The buggers are all over out there. We're losing this one. Shouldn't we pull back?"

Loomis was tempted. But in retreating out of the gorge the monks would be exposed. Casualties would be high. Loomis checked his watch. Lhalde should be starting the climb over the first pass. He needed only a little more time.

"It's only an hour or so before dark," he said. "We'll wait until then to make our move."

"What move?" Owenby asked.

"I'll think of something," Loomis said.

Oztrak crawled forward through the grass until he was beside Erbakan, their faces almost touching.

"Why have you stopped moving forward?" he demanded. "What's wrong with you?"

"It's suicide, my commander," Erbakan said. "They shoot at anything that moves."

Oztrak glanced upward. His flankers were still in place, pouring bullets down on the monks. He had Loomis pinned down, unable to move. The battle was in stalemate. But Oztrak was impatient. With every minute that passed, Lhalde and his caravan were traveling deeper into the mountains.

"Get your men up on their feet," Oztrak ordered. "Charge the monks and destroy them."

Erbakan's mouth worked twice before he managed to speak.

"But, my commander! We would lose many men!"

"No one said this would be easy," Oztrak said, holding his temper in check. "Naturally we will lose men. But they have pledged their lives and now the moment has come for them to make good on their promise. Some will fall. But others will reach the monks and destroy them."

Erbakan did not answer. His face appeared unusually pale, even against the sun-bleached dry grass.

"Issue the order. Now!" Oztrak said.

The men had practiced the maneuver of rising and charging on foot many times back in training under Gungor, Pishan, and Erek. Oztrak had always operated on the theory that if a procedure was repeated often enough, it would be performed automatically in the heat of battle.

"Move!" he said.

Erbakan turned and shouted orders for a charge. He gathered his feet and hands beneath him and paused for a long moment.

"Go!" he shouted.

Erbakan and perhaps two-thirds of his men rose out of the grass and ran toward the line of monks, firing as they went, awkwardly working the bolts of their rifles. Within seconds a barrage of return fire from the monks began taking a terrible toll. The meat-cleaver sounds of bullets striking flesh were unmistakable. Men dropped all around Oztrak.

For an exhilarating moment he thought the charge would be successful. A few of his men actually reached the strange rock formation where the monks were concealed. But at that crucial point the charge faltered under a renewed barrage from the monks. Within seconds more than a dozen of his Uighurs fell. The dwindling rank broke. The survivors turned and fled back to the safety of the grass.

Erbakan crawled back to Oztrak. He was weeping.

"We tried, my commander. You saw what happened."

His tears began to flow freely. Oztrak put a hand to his shoulder.

"Control yourself," he said. "I'm ordering up replacements. When they arrive, you will try again."

"Pass the word to give me covering fire," Loomis said. "When I'm finished, we'll fall back by the numbers."

"More likely you'll get your killing," Owenby said. "Then what the hell will the rest of us do?"

"Won't happen," Loomis said. "But if it should, just fall back without me."

Darkness was coming faster than Loomis expected. Ahead, details of the walls of the gorge already were indistinct. He hoped the snipers up there were experiencing the same difficulty in seeing the ground below.

He left his rifle leaning against the limestone block and carried his .380 Belgian semiautomatic in his hand, cocked and locked. Carefully he strapped the bag of gunpowder to his shoulders.

"Will that be enough?" Owenby asked.

"If it isn't, then the idea won't work," Loomis said. "Give me three minutes. Then start the covering fire."

Owenby checked his watch, then crawled away. A moment later Loomis heard him conveying his instructions in Tibetan.

Cautiously, Loomis inched his way into the grass.

During the last hour the warrior monks had turned back two Uighur charges. Both had carried right up to the monks' line of defense before breaking. Loomis had lost two more monks—one killed and one wounded. Dead Uighurs littered the ground. Loomis crawled among them, moving slowly, trying not to make a telltale ripple in the grass that might be observed either by the snipers above or the other Uighurs below.

He reached the edge of the small, frozen stream. Cautiously he uncorked the bag of gunpowder and began laying a trail through the grass. He took his time, making certain the chain of powder was unbroken.

The covering fire began on schedule, offering the Uighurs diversion while Loomis crawled across the most vulnerable portion of the battlefield.

Each time he encountered a body, he worked his way around it. Even above the gunfire he could hear the sonic snap of bullets passing less than a yard over his head.

The gunpowder lasted for more than fifty yards. When the sack was empty, Loomis reached into the pockets of his sheepskin coat for matches. Cupping his hand to protect the flame from the strong breeze and to prevent its being seen from above, he lit the end of the train of gunpowder.

Lofting six inches high, the flame began its course across the battlefield, igniting grass as it went.

Shouts came from the Uighur lines as they saw what was happening. The grass blazed up, lighting the walls of the gorge.

Hurriedly Loomis crawled several yards away from the flames before rising to his feet. Running in a half crouch, he reached the safety of the tilted limestone.

Pausing only to retrieve his rifle, he followed the monks up the slope. The Uighurs were shooting in an attempt to stop the retreat, but the range was long and the burning grass provided an effective screen. Not a man was hit as the monks scrambled over the hill to where the yaks waited.

From behind them came more shouting as the Uighurs fled the wind-whipped flames and a few screams from the wounded on the battlefield, in recognition that soon they would be burned alive.

Loomis, Owenby, and the monks rode up the trail in deepening darkness, moving slowly, trusting the yaks to find the way.

Two hours later they reached the foot of the climb up to the first high pass. There the wounded man died.

"They have thirty minutes to bury him," Loomis told Owenby. "When they're through, we'll start the climb."

"Tonight? You're daft!" Owenby said. "We can't go up there in the dark!"

Loomis had been studying the ground.

"Lhalde's yaks went up in single file. They left a well-worn trail. Our yaks shouldn't have any trouble following them."

"It'll be forty degrees colder up there in the pass," Owenby argued.

"Can't be helped," Loomis said. "We don't want to get caught here in the morning and go up with Oztrak taking potshots at us all the way."

The painstaking climb took most of the night. But once they reached the pass, they managed three hours of sleep before dawn.

For a time Loomis considered making another stand in the pass. But the defensive position was not good, and he felt he should not let the caravan get too far ahead of the warrior monks. So they pushed on, descending from the pass on a narrow shelf that hung over a spectacular chasm.

They caught up with the caravan just before noon. Lhalde came to meet them. His face was drawn with exhaustion and worry. He asked about the battle and Loomis gave him a brief summary.

"I was hoping you'd be farther along," Loomis said. "Oztrak can't be far behind us."

Lhalde seemed discouraged.

"The yaks are suffering from hard use and the altitude," he said. "They can't last much longer."

"We'll just do the best we can," Loomis said. "But we must push on."

Yet he, too, was appalled at the slow pace as the caravan resumed its journey. The yaks would stop and refuse to budge until goaded. Each time one stopped, all behind him stopped in domino fashion.

The caravan was moving more slowly than a man would if he were walking leisurely. Loomis could not think of a way to move the caravan faster. Aware that Oztrak might come upon them at any moment, he kept the warrior monks at the rear of the caravan, ready for instant action.

In later afternoon, during a brief halt to feed the yaks, the Kamala Lama sent for Loomis. Bundled heavily against the cold, he had left his palanquin and was walking up and down beside it for exercise. He stopped and faced Loomis.

"I want you to know I consider that you have fulfilled your contract with the lamasery," he said. "You have trained the warrior monks well and led them to do more than we had any right to expect. I'm most grateful."

Loomis remained silent, wondering why the lama had chosen this moment to make the announcement. He did not have to wait long for the answer.

"You remember my priorities, I hope," the lama said. "The safety of the library is paramount. Therefore, if it becomes necessary, I may order the warrior monks to fall back and make an heroic last stand while the caravan escapes. I know this sounds harsh and unfeeling, especially to Western ears. But the human soul is durable. It cannot be destroyed. Truth, regrettably, is fragile and forever must be protected and preserved."

The lama hesitated, looking at Loomis as if anticipating a response. Loomis offered none.

"So if I order the warrior monks to fall back for a final stand, I don't expect you to be with them," the lama continued. "I am relieving you of all obligations."

Loomis did not even consider the suggestion.

"I won't abandon men I trained," he said. "That's not the way I do business."

The Kamala Lama frowned. "I regret you feel compelled. I emphasize that it is your choice."

Without answering, Loomis turned and walked away. The caravan moved on.

Late in the afternoon they climbed the second pass, into the most spectacular region of the most rugged mountains on earth. Snow-mantled peaks soared all around them. They traversed a high shelf, hanging over an awesome abyss.

It was there Oztrak caught up with them.

At first the Uighurs were only a speck of movement on the shelf, far behind. But they came on relentlessly, constantly gaining ground. Owenby studied them through his binoculars.

"The buggers have given up on their horses," he said. "They're on foot and moving at a good clip. They could *crawl* and overtake these bloody yaks."

Loomis searched for a good place to make another defensive stand. For the most part the wall above the shelf was sheer, offering no cover. But with the Uighurs less than a half mile away, the caravan at last came to a section of the shelf where the rock wall had split, showering boulders down on the shelf.

"We'll make a stand here," Loomis said. "Before the caravan is too far ahead, we'll fall back."

Owenby explained the strategy to the monks. Hurriedly, Loomis assigned them to their positions.

"You don't have to stay," Loomis told Owenby. "The Kamala Lama has released us from our contract. The monks know what to do. I won't need an interpreter."

"Maybe not," Owenby said. "But you sure as shit need another rifle. I'll stay, if you don't mind."

Loomis slapped him on the back. Owenby selected a boulder, sprawled behind it, removed his right glove, and began laying out ammunition.

"Now why the fuck did I say that?" he asked. "I'm Bertrand P. Owenby, the well-known coward."

He slipped his bare hand under his coat to protect it from the cold as long as possible. He laughed.

"This change of heart comes at a most inconvenient time, old sod," he said to Loomis. "I had just figured out how I can take the money from this jolly little stroll and buy my way back into the world. Now all my scheming may very well come to naught."

Loomis did not answer. Oztrak's army, still more than two hundred strong, was coming within range.

And Loomis had only twenty-seven rifles to stop them.

Wary, Oztrak approached the fallen boulders with caution. The landslide seemed exactly the type of place Loomis would choose to make a stand. So he was not surprised by the first barrage of rifle fire.

"Down!" he shouted. "Shoot into the crevices."

His men obeyed. Although the monks could not be seen from the distance, Oztrak knew that bullets fired into the crevices would ricochet, spraying shards of rock and lead. Although his men were exposed out on the naked shelf, steady fire from their two hundred and twenty-four rifles kept the monks down behind the boulders. The roar of their guns echoed again and again off the surrounding mountains, growing in volume until the whole world seemed concentrated on this firefight.

Oztrak crawled forward until he reached Erbakan, who lay directing the fire. In the distance, at a place where the shelf curved, the caravan again came into view. It moved so slowly that Oztrak had to watch it for a time to make certain it was moving at all.

"The caravan is escaping," Erbakan said. He fired a shot at the caravan, even though it was well out of range.

"Let them go," Oztrak said. "Keep the pressure on the monks."

By comparison, the return fire from the monks seemed weak and ineffective.

Oztrak was satisfied. If he failed to overwhelm Loomis's dwindling defense in this firefight, he would in the next, or perhaps in the one after that.

20

One by one, the monks fell back, hurrying to put distance between themselves and the Uighur guns. Owenby came running to Loomis.

"Four dead, three wounded," he said.

Loomis squeezed off three more shots to keep the Uighurs at bay. Then he and Owenby ran after the retreating monks.

After a hundred yards, the shelf offered protection. Loomis and Owenby stopped for breath.

"What the fuck will we do now?" Owenby asked. "In case it escaped your attention, they almost wiped us out back there."

Loomis did not answer. He was down to twenty riflemen, counting himself and Owenby. The firefight had been woefully one-sided. The Uighur shooting had been constant and expert. Loomis doubted that the monks could survive another such onslaught.

"Get the wounded men forward to the caravan," he said. "I'll hunt another place. We'll make another stand."

Owenby shook his head in dismay and moved forward to convey Loomis's orders.

Loomis brought up the rear of the retreat, while searching the shelf ahead for even the slightest protection. He found none.

Even in delayed retreat, Loomis and the monks soon came upon the caravan. Loomis glanced back. The Uighurs were coming on relentlessly.

Lhalde dropped back to confer with Loomis.

"We simply can't go much farther without resting," he said. "The yaks are staggering. Soon they'll start dying."

Behind them, some of the monks began swapping shots with the Uighurs, even though the range was too long. The rifle fire echoed off the mountains and came back magnified as a sustained roar.

"And I'm worried about that," Lhalde said, gesturing to the sound. "The snow bridge is just ahead. The gunfire may bring it down on us when we try to pass beneath it."

"How far ahead?" Loomis asked.

"The maps show it around the next curve. Perhaps a mile from here."

Loomis seized upon the first glimmer of a plan and nurtured it. He called to Owenby.

"Where's Drupa?"

"Up ahead, with his yaks," Owenby said.

"Send him to me. And tell Khedru and his monks we'll make another stand here and start falling back a hundred yards at a time in a running firefight. We must buy time for the caravan to get past the snow bridge."

"Oh, my God," Owenby said. "The fucking gunfire will bring it down, sure as shit."

"Maybe not," Loomis said. "Lhalde, move the caravan on past the snow bridge. You can stop on the other side, if you must, and we'll make a hard stand there."

And the final one, he thought, if his plan failed.

Lhalde hurried forward to get the caravan moving again. Khedru and his men gathered. Through Owenby, Loomis described how he wanted them to kneel and fire, then fall back, time after time, to keep the Uighurs at a distance.

"What about Drupa?" Owenby asked.

"Tell him to keep close. We'll be needing him."

The Uighurs were coming within range. Loomis positioned his men, waited for the right moment, then ordered them to fire.

After emptying their rifles, they fell back a hundred yards, re-formed, and again waited for his order.

Repeating the maneuver time after time, they retreated around a long curve of the shelf until the snow bridge came into view.

It hung over a horseshoe curve of the shelf, over a deep abyss. Emerald green from the ice at its base, the snowbridge had been a threat to travelers for centuries. It was marked as a hazard on the oldest maps in the lamasery library. Mesmerized, Loomis and his men stared at it in awe.

"The fucking gunfire will bring it down," Owenby predicted. "So we're screwed any way we play our cards."

"I have a hunch it's sturdier than it looks," Loomis said. "It's been there for a thousand years."

"Gathering snow all that time," Owenby said. "Which means the fucker's long past due to fall."

"Send for Drupa," Loomis said.

While the warrior monks made yet another stand, Loomis led Drupa and Owenby to a vantage point where they could see the entire length of the snow bridge.

"Ask Drupa if he thinks he can place charges at each end and bring it down," Loomis said to Owenby. "Long fuses, giving him plenty of time to get down and for us to retreat past it."

"But not time enough for the Uighurs," Owenby said, grasping the plan. "Holy shit. It might work. If the fucker doesn't come down on us from the gunfire."

That was a risk, but one that had to be taken.

"Ask him," Loomis said.

Owenby and Drupa talked hurriedly and at length. Drupa was smiling. Loomis waited.

"He says he's sure he can bring it down," Owenby summarized. "It'll take the last of his blasting powder, but he can do it."

"Give him your watch," Loomis said. "We'll time it exactly."

Owenby pushed back his coat and removed his wristwatch. But Drupa refused to take it.

"He says he'll follow our movements from up there and time it visually," Owenby explained.

"Give him the watch," Loomis said. "We can't fuck up by a single minute."

At last, Drupa succumbed to Owenby's argument, shrugged, and took the watch. He loaded the gunpowder and detonators on his back and began climbing.

Loomis found an outcrop and the monks made a longer, more sustained stand, buying time for the caravan, and for Drupa.

As the roar of gunfire continued to resound and echo off the mountains, the caravan moved with agonizing slowness under the snow bridge. Despite his belief that the massive pile of ice and snow was sturdier than it looked, Loomis still found himself holding his breath, waiting for the first sign of movement indicating the start of a horrendous avalanche that would bury the entire caravan.

Yet the gunfire could not be diminished. Time after time the monks made a brief stand, then retreated. Even at maximum range, the return fire from the Uighurs was deadly. Four more monks fell—two dead and two wounded. Both of the wounded men insisted on remaining at their posts.

Loomis monitored Drupa as he made his way up more than a thousand feet to the overhang of ice. As the monks gradually fell back, he placed his charges.

Slowly the caravan made its way out of the danger zone. Again the monks retreated, made another stand.

Loomis was worried about the timing. He remembered that the fuses on the charges to seal the lamasery had been inaccurate. The first had gone off a full two minutes too late, allowing some of the Uighurs to escape. The second had gone off too soon, not allowing Loomis sufficient time to get well clear.

This one had to be more accurate. A minute too soon, and Loomis and his retreating warrior monks would be trapped under the avalanche. A minute too late, and the Uighurs would make their way safely past the snow bridge before it fell. After that the Uighurs would be free to make short work of the surviving warrior monks and of the caravan itself.

Slowly, buying the caravan and Drupa more time, Loomis and the monks retreated to a point beneath the overhang.

Owenby watched Drupa through binoculars.

"He's signaling," Owenby said. "He's pointing to my watch and motioning us on. He's telling us it's time to haul ass."

Loomis checked his watch. The signal was two minutes too soon. Apparently Drupa had already lit the fuses.

Loomis hesitated but briefly. Drupa was in a much better position to judge.

"Tell the men to fall back," Loomis said. "We'll try to hold them once they get directly under the snow bridge."

Hurriedly they retreated. Two more monks fell. One was killed instantly, his skull pierced. The other took a bullet through his chest. Loomis shouldered him and followed the monks beneath the overhang.

Struggling under his burden, Loomis could think of nothing else but the fact that the fuses were burning and that in scant moments an entire side of the mountain would come down. Out of breath, he staggered under the load of the wounded man. Ahead, Owenby glanced back, saw him, and came to help. Together they carried the wounded monk another hundred yards. There he was taken by other hands.

In the retreat Loomis had lost his perspective of exactly where the danger zone lay. He walked to the edge of the abyss and looked up. The snow bridge was partially obscured, but he regained a sense of its location.

"Another eighty yards," he said to Owenby. "Then we'll make our stand."

Owenby glanced up. "Too bloody close," he said. "I'd make it two hundred yards."

"We don't want Oztrak past the overhang," Loomis said.

He could not find a good position, so they took up their stand on the bare shelf. The Uighurs were coming fast, now obviously aware of the danger.

"Fire!" Loomis ordered through Owenby. "Give them everything you've got!"

Whether the order gained or lost in translation Loomis did not know. But the remaining monks worked their rifle bolts furiously, pouring bullets into Oztrak's advancing army.

In panic, the Uighurs refused to be delayed. They came on into the withering fire.

Loomis knew his men could not hold them.

He was tempted to order yet another retreat, but he shoved the thought from his mind. He was committed. Whether the final stand was made here or later, the results would be the same. He fired into the advancing Uighurs with abandon, convinced that the Kamala Lama's warrior monks were making their final stand.

Then came a roar that blocked all the senses. It came from above and continued to grow in volume.

Out on the shelf, the Uighurs broke formation. Some ran forward desperately. Others turned and ran back. Only a moment later the scene was swept from sight by a curtain of white.

The sound was like the end of the world as the snows of a thousand years poured over the shelf and into the abyss. Gale-force winds swept out, threatening to knock Loomis and the monks from their feet.

The cataclysmic roar continued for two full minutes. The sound echoed throughout the mountains, then died away to a stunningly profound silence.

Owenby was the first to speak.

"Where's Drupa?"

Loomis knew. He did not know how he knew, but he

knew. He remembered the way Drupa had refused the watch and how he had been so confident of the timing.

"He used short fuses," he explained. "He went with the avalanche."

Owenby walked over and gazed into the abyss.

"Well, I suppose that's the last we'll see of Oztrak."

"In this lifetime," Loomis said.

Owenby rolled his eyes skyward.

Bone-weary, Loomis walked toward the caravan, his bed, and a good night of sleep. He was still adjusting to the fact that the danger was past.

Now he and the caravan had only to cross on over the backbone of the world and descend to the headwaters of the Ganges, and the safety of India.